HUMAN SACRIFICE

Sheriff went back inside the temple.

Roger wasn't where he'd been told to wait.

With the noise of the helicopter suddenly gone, the place seemed ominously silent.

"Roger!" Sheriff called, quietly, for the temple was small.

"Here . . ." he heard a reply: soft, strained.

Sheriff went that way. He passed a small aperture where a portion of a wall had toppled, and saw Roger in a small stone chamber on the other side.

Alone, but looking down at something.

Michael stepped over the rubble, and moved beside his son. Roger was standing in front of a hewn stone the size of a breakfast-room table.

An altar.

On that altar, hidden in an inner chamber of a ruined temple in the middle of one of the densest tropical forests on Earth, lay four human hearts, so fresh that the blood that had spilled out of the filled arteries still lay in uncoagulated pools on the corrugated surface of the stone . . .

MICHAEL SHERIFF: THE SHIELD

ISLAND INTRIGUE

PRESTON MacADAM

AVON
PUBLISHERS OF BARD, CAMELOT, DISCUS AND FLARE BOOKS

AVON BOOKS
A division of
The Hearst Corporation
1790 Broadway
New York, New York 10019

Copyright © 1985 by Preston MacAdam
Published by arrangement with the author
Library of Congress Catalog Card Number: 84-91779
ISBN: 0-380-89689-3

First Avon Printing, September 1985

AVON TRADEMARK REG. U. S. PAT. OFF. AND IN OTHER
COUNTRIES, MARCA REGISTRADA, HECHO EN U. S. A.

Printed in the U. S. A.

WFH 10 9 8 7 6 5 4 3 2 1

For Mr. Bender

IT WAS A COLD afternoon in November, the Saturday right after Thanksgiving. Nineteen-year-old Roger Sheriff was walking aimlessly through downtown Boston. He was supposed to begin his Christmas shopping today.

The people in Boston didn't even make a pretense at Christmas cheer. The inhabitants of the city took the holiday as an excuse to be more hurried, more harried, and ruder than they were at other times—which was pretty damn hurried, harried, and rude.

Roger Sheriff took one look at the huge crowds that were forcing their way toward the downtown shopping area and moved in the opposite direction. He wasn't ready for them. He'd take a walk through the Boston Common, hoping it would help him build up the energy to face that mob. He wasn't ready for that many people right now.

He followed one of the meandering pathways through the Common until he came to an empty park bench. The New England air was brisk, but the bright sunlight offered some hope for warmth.

Roger sat down and slumped against the back of the seat. He closed his eyes and leaned his head backward. The sun did feel good. He felt so much older than just nineteen. This fit, he told himself with a smirk—it was just what he should be doing, sitting on a park bench like he was some kind of geriatric case.

A shadow fell across his face. He opened his eyes.

Three kids about Roger's age stood there. Since moving to Boston, Roger had learned the type. They were all bulky, but young enough that their bulk had some strength to it. In another ten years it would all be three masses of beer belly. Now they could still make believe they were macho studs. That would pass.

Roger also recognized the stance. Threatening.

"Don't even think about it," Roger said. His voice sounded tired.

The three teenagers grinned. "Hey, come on, man," said the one closest to him. "What're you talking about? We just came over to be friendly."

"Friendly with a piece in your jacket," said Roger. The kid's right hand was tucked away in the pocket of a South Boston High School letter jacket. Probably lettered in football and armed robbery.

"Hey man, it's a dangerous city. Never know what kind of shit you run across in the street. Them Combat Zone niggers got no morals at all. Got to carry a little protection."

All three of them laughed.

"Get lost, asshole," said Roger quietly.

"Don't talk to my buddy that way." The one standing in back was the ugliest. His complexion was a disaster. "You'll get him mad."

Roger took in the situation calmly. Each of the three had some sort of weapon in his pocket. Each of the three had his hand on that weapon. A distinct advantage—for Roger.

"Look, I'll tell you what," he said. "I'll warn you once. I'm in much better shape than you are. I have skills you don't. I can do things you wouldn't believe if you saw them, and wouldn't understand if I explained. So why don't the three of you go mug somebody else?"

"Hey look," said the leader, the one in front, "we're just out Christmas shopping. For our mothers. Our mothers get disappointed if there's nothing under the tree on Christmas morning. Yeah, and we also want to donate to the IRA. We got to help support the freedom fighters in Northern Ireland.''

''Yeah,'' agreed the other in front. ''Gotta buy presents and gotta give to the IRA.''

''So why don't you help us out?'' said the one in back. ''Give us a little something.''

''Like everything you got in your wallet,'' added the leader.

Roger had already looked around. No one was near. Boylston Street was just on the other side of the little graveyard, and there were people walking there, but they probably couldn't have heard him if he'd called for help. And if they'd heard him, they probably wouldn't come. People in Boston have seen a fair amount of violence on the streets. They don't interfere—they just get out of the way and go on with their business. And tell a cop if they happen to run into one. Nobody would come if Roger called.

Roger would have liked just to call out for help. Not for his own sake, but for the sake of these three hoodlums. Because now they were going to have to deal with him alone.

One more time he'd try. ''Just leave me alone, okay?''

''I want your money, faggot. *Now.* '' The leader of the Irish kids slapped out a hand and struck Roger's face hard. It was an earnest show of the damage he'd do if provoked further, and a demonstration of the lack of fear he had of possible witnesses.

I tried, Roger thought before instinct and training took over.

The three hands were still holding the weapons in pockets. Each of the men was at a certain distance that Roger's eye calculated precisely.

Roger's legs struck out with a ferocity that was blindingly swift and unexpected. The two men in front were caught in the groin, and they staggered backward, exposing the man in the middle.

Roger's feet were now on the ground. His body hurtled

forward and he smashed head-first into the third man's belly.

Whooooosh.

That was the air expelled forcibly from the guy's chest.

Roger straightened himself. The two whose groins he'd kicked were bent over, staggering in tight circles. He fisted his hands and employed them as hammers, driving each of the men down with blows to the back of the neck.

If he had hit differently, with the edge of his hand rather than his fist, he might have killed them with these blows. As it was, each man fell hard onto the sidewalk. One crushed his nose—Roger could tell from the gush of blood that spewed out from that part of his face. The other's skull crunched aloud when it made contact. Probably a contusion.

The third man was vomiting his lunch, holding his belly as if afraid that his intestines would spill out onto the ground.

Roger glanced at the three of them with disgust, and then simply strolled away. These three weren't even worth a parting insult.

Roger walked through the park until he got to Tremont Street, the fast-moving thoroughfare that separates the Common from the center of Boston. After crossing Tremont, he moved up one of the many side streets that would take him to Downtown Crossing, the intense retail shopping area. He studied faces as he walked the center of the pedestrianized brick street. Many looked back. *What did they see?* he wondered. He caught a glimpse of his own reflection in a mirror set up in a clothing store that catered to pimps.

I look so normal!

He looked a little older than his age. His dark brown hair was carefully cut in a short military style. His clothes were good-looking—they should be. They cost a fucking fortune. He wasn't quite his father's six-foot height, but he was getting there. He suspected he'd make it soon, one last spurt of growth before he stabilized.

A small, wimpish-looking man hollered apologies when Roger barged into him on the sidewalk. The thought of how much he was beginning to resemble his father had produced a snarl on Roger's face so intense that the man had decided to take immediate blame for the accident.

Roger kept on his way. He was more conscious of his body these days than he ever had been before. He had to be. He'd put himself through grueling training since moving to Massachusetts eighteen months ago. At first he'd done it to earn his father's approval. Then he'd kept it up as a brutal form of competition with his old man. Now? Now he did it to stay alive.

His arms were bulky from weightlifting, his thighs from running. His waist had actually shrunk as his abdominal muscles had taken on new tone. He sneered again. *I'm a mean mother-fucker.* That's what the stupid jocks back home in Nevada had said when they described their own abilities and achievements in the weight room. What assholes. Those muscles of theirs were for bulk or for show or some inane sense of self-satisfaction—they were the masculine equivalent of siliconed tits. Roger was developing his own body for an entirely more realistic reason: His body was the principal tool in his work.

He thought about his father. They had had a fight this morning. The same one; it distressed Roger. He'd had too many of these run-ins and he knew there was no good reason for them. He and his father were on edge. The two of them were caught in a net—the same net—and when they struggled to get out of it, they just ended up hitting one another.

Just the fact that they were together would have been enough to create problems, Roger figured. It had been years—many years—since the two of them had had anything to do with one another. But then Roger had made his decision on his eighteenth birthday. He wanted to know what it would be like to have a father. The life he was leading in Reno was a dead-end street. His friends and acquaintances were on the way down, the slow, winding way down to meaningless lives and meaningless jobs, or else they were on a very straight, very fast road to the state pen.

There was nothing in Nevada to keep him from taking one road or the other. His mother's love affair with her bottle and the revolving door she kept on her bedroom weren't exactly stabilizing influences, as the guidance counselors used to say.

Then he'd gotten the note. It was strange. Just a simple folded page telling him Michael Sheriff's address in Sudbury, Massachusetts. Roger made believe that it was an invitation from his dad. He wanted to believe that. He'd climbed into his clunker and driven across country, hardly ever stopping.

What he found when he got to Massachusetts was beyond what he'd ever imagined. There had always been checks in the mail and, because of the way his mother framed her financial complaints, Roger had figured that they were fairly large. There was never any worry about food, rent—or booze. So it made sense that his father was well-off. But that was an understatement.

To begin with, there was the house: one of those pre-Revolutionary things that all these New Englanders made so much fuss about. It was two hundred years old, and it made Nevada construction techniques look like cardboard-and-Scotch tape. Three stories, rambling, with fireplaces in a dozen rooms, every one of them big enough to hold half a log. And enough acreage surrounding the place that the only people who knew it was there were those who flew right over it in a 'copter.

At first Roger had been disappointed in his father's car—just a gray Volvo Turbo. But then Roger found out how that thing ran. And discovered it was armor-plated, with bulletproofed windows. And eventually he learned what was most important about that car—when it was driving down a road in Massachusetts, nobody gave it a second glance. Lesson learned: The rich spend money for anonymity, not for show.

So Roger had come to Massachusetts on a quest for some *father* to give him direction. It was an adolescent fantasy, a Hollywood plot: teenager set adrift in the modern, valueless land and then, miraculously, saved by some godlike paternal figure who gives him guidance and a sense of self-worth.

Well, Michael Sheriff had certainly given Roger direction. Roger clenched his fist hard enough to feel his nails digging at his palms. He sure as hell had given Roger a lot of *direction*.

It had been dreamlike. The house, the money, the stud car his father had bought him, all of it. There was even mystery in the way that Michael Sheriff made his money. There was this firm, MIS. Management Information Services. It had a big expensive building out on Route 128. Millions of people passed it as they drove that eight-lane road, the Highway of American Technology. They all probably figured that it was just another strange and profitable high-tech firm that was just like all the others in that scientific mecca.

MIS wasn't just another high-tech firm, though—far from it.

Management Information Services was in a class by itself. Headed by the Chairman—he had no other name that anybody knew of—it was the bastion of decency in the world. So it claimed. It was the court of last resort for the forces that would fight evil and protect good—for a price. It was . . .

It had seemed so wonderful to Roger. The old man, the Chairman, had doted on him. Sure, so Dad went off on some weird assignment in Africa. When he came back he'd been a basket case, all kinds of crap had come out about the nature of man and his society. Michael Sheriff had gone a little bonkers. He'd tried to explain to Roger why. How he'd found in himself, during that assign-

ment, a kernel of the barbarian that terrified him. He had
found some primeval self under the layers of Western
civilization that simply didn't fit with anything else, at
least not with anything else that Michael Sheriff had
wanted to admit.

But his father had come out of it. They had picked up
their training again. The hard runs in the morning, the
workouts in the gym, the daily swims in the pool. It was
part of the dream, their dreams of being father-to-the-son
and son-to-the-father, a dream of forgetting the years of
separation.

Then Roger had fucked it up, but good. He had never
honestly told Michael about the conversations he'd had
with the Chairman while Michael was away. But the
mystery of it all had gotten to Roger, the allure had been
too great.

He had discovered more details about his father and his
father's life. He learned, for one thing, just how much
money Michael did make. A whole fucking lot more than
Roger had even dreamed. He found out other things, too.
That it had been the Chairman who had sent him that note
with the directions to the Massachusetts house. He had
done it because he wanted Roger to follow his father's
footsteps. He wanted Roger to sign up with MIS. The son
would be bound to his father not only by blood and by af-
fection, but as an apprentice. He'd study at highbrow
Breslauer University while the training progressed. When
he was finished with his studies he could move right into
the organization.

Michael Sheriff had been bullshit when he "uncovered
the plot." He'd felt . . .

Roger now understood many of his father's emotions.
He hadn't at the time, but now they made sense. Michael
Sheriff felt betrayed, as though Roger and the Chairman
had gone behind his back in some way. That, and he simply and purely didn't want Roger to become like himself.

It was, at least partially, the experience in Africa. Michael didn't want Roger to find that kernel of barbarism

in himself. But Roger *had* found it, and even now it was so real he could feel it rolling around—round and hard and cold—in his belly.

That was only a few months ago—last summer. So much had happened since—he was so different now; yet so much remained the same. Now, on a side street in Boston in November with his wallet full of money for Christmas presents, he felt alone and vulnerable.

"Do you know what?" Roger stood in front of his father, almost at parade rest.

Michael Sheriff sat deep in a massive leather chair near the fire in the living room. Open on his lap was a new book on New England architecture. He looked up at his son, and then glanced down at the floor.

"Yes. I know that you didn't take off your boots when you came in, so you've tracked snow through the house."

Roger stiffened.

Here we go again, Michael thought. He was immediately sorry about the cutting remark, but he was still feeling the residue of the argument they'd had that morning. Why did he always speak so quickly—and always, it seemed, to belittle Roger? Damn! He waited for the all-too-predictable explosion. None came. Instead, Roger seemed to will himself to relax.

Michael Sheriff watched his son's shoulders sag in a small but very apparent act of submission.

"I've never spent Christmas with you before," Roger said quietly.

"When you were a baby . . ." Michael answered automatically, having no idea what Roger's intention was. He suspected a trap.

"That's not what I mean. I mean, since I was a kid, you've never been around on the holidays."

Not an accusation, just a statement of fact. But Michael was still waiting for Roger to shift gears, to turn the statement of fact into a weapon. Michael waited impatiently. If the little bastard thought—

"I want to do it right," Roger said.

Michael was surprised. He now realized this wasn't an attack, and wasn't going to turn into one. Christ, the kid was practically waving a white flag. And Jesus, they had to stop this constant bickering. The house had turned into an armed camp over the past few months. Ever since the incident with that Israeli girl . . .

"I thought we were doing it right," said Michael carefully. "I mean, Christmas. Here, in the house. Our house," he corrected himself. "We'll be together."

"We'll be together with our own spy taking infrared photographs of Santa Claus coming down the chimney. Hiding in the kitchen and taking inventory of the goddamn presents. That is, if she's not on assignment Christmas morning, blowing up Khadaffy's house or something."

"Roger . . ."

But Roger was right of course. Katrina, their housekeeper, *was* a spy. And she probably would take notes on the gifts, and turn the notes over to the Chairman for evaluation.

Michael Sheriff had suffered the presence of Katrina since he'd moved into this house. He had lived with the knowledge that MIS could never totally trust any one of its employees, not even its principal agent, Michael Sheriff.

An agent could be under quiet stress that would lead to disaster in the field. Family problems, drinking, even drugs were possible. And, it seemed, every agent had a secret. One thing, small or large, that could be employed for purposes of blackmail.

Katrina was Sheriff's counterweight. She looked like the perfect household servant—Nordic, asexual, physically attractive, with a frigid manner. She was an excel-

lent cook, and kept the house spotless. But she was also
the eyes of MIS in Michael Sheriff's home. So long as
Michael and Roger knew that their lives were being led in
a manner that would not worry the agency, they needn't
feel concern. But both father and son knew that their recent bickering had been reported—and that, in fact, it
should have been, because it was affecting both of
them.

Once an agent for the Swedish secret service, Katrina
had found the placid neutrality of her homeland an unac-
ceptable brake on the practice of her greatest skill—
assassination. She was the long arm of MIS when the
quick, quiet, and mysterious elimination of a single enemy was the optimal method of action.

She sometimes disappeared for a few days, merely
leaving a note on the door of the refrigerator reading, ''I
will return.'' Over the next few days, Michael and Roger
would quietly scour the many newspapers that came
through their hands to find the one unlikely, sudden, or
strange death. The blood that was spilled was by Katrina's spotlessly white hands.

It was impossible not to feel resentment for a spy in the
house, and it was equally impossible not to accept her
presence. It was a precondition to employment for both
Michael and his son.

''Look,'' said Roger, with a kind of desperation in his
voice. ''Can we compromise?''

Michael Sheriff put down his book. ''Compromise
about what?''

''Look, I know this house is important to you. I *like*
the house. I *love* the house. But, it's the holidays. You
know? And . . .'' Roger faltered. He moved through the
living room with his arms in motion, obviously trying to
get something out that would break through the walls that
had been erected between him and his father. But he was
up against an obstacle now that made his speech difficult
and halting.

Come on, kid, you can do it. Michael was desperate for his son to continue.

"I want to spend some time with my *father.*"

Roger put his hands to his face and Michael was stunned to think that his son was going to cry. But he wasn't. He took the palms away from his eyes and looked at Michael. "I came out here, back East, to find my *father.* I found . . . *you.* I . . . love you.' Really, I do. But . . . I was thinking today, in the city. These things came over me, you know? Then these three guys tried to jump me. I wiped them out. I just wiped them *out.* And then I turned around and I was looking at them on the ground, and I'm thinking, 'Oh God, I'm only nineteen years old . . .' I just want to be a regular guy some-times."

Michael started to speak, but Roger wouldn't let him. He jumped right in: "It's *my* fault, I know it. Don't start on me. I'm the one who joined MIS behind your back. Okay? All of it, I know, all of it is my fault."

Michael didn't say anything. He suspected there was more. There was.

"But I'm still only nineteen. And sometimes I want to pretend that that's *all* that I am. Just a regular nineteen-year-old guy who's living with his father. But look what we do together: We train. You teach me handguns and assault weapons. We train: You teach me survival meth-ods and strategy. We walk down the street and you show me how to know which guys are armed. We go to a thea-ter and you lecture me on sightlines, and we pretend there's going to be an assassination and I have to figure out where the assassin is sitting. We go to the beach and you show me where amphibious forces would land. We go—"

"I get the message." Michael Sheriff studied his son. "I don't know what to say. Roger, you *did* choose this life. You do have to take responsibility for that. Now you're in it. You're in MIS up to your asshole. I have to teach you those things if you're going to survive. I don't *like* it—showing you all that shit. But I have to, because I think—I *know*—that one day you're going to come up against something, and you'd better be prepared. Because if you're not prepared, you're dead. And then I'm going to come along and find your body, and I'm going to say to myself, 'He's dead because I didn't train him properly.' And that's not going to happen.''

Roger was still, standing with his back to the fire. Thinking about what his father had said, he was silent.

"I feel like I'm running a race, Roger. I've felt that way ever since I heard you were part of the operation. I want you to know everything I know and I want you to be able to do everything I can do, and I will not apologize for that. The simplest MIS operation can turn into something enormously complex and difficult. What I teach you is what is going to keep you alive. Do you understand? Do you really understand?''

"I do," Roger said simply. "And I also understand that my attitude has been bad. I know I can't change overnight, but I *can* change. And I'm *going* to change. But can't we—"

"Can't we what?''

"Can't we have a vacation? I mean, a vacation where we made believe we were just a guy and his son? Can't we go somewhere? I have time now. In a couple of weeks I'll be finished with classes. We get a month's vacation. Let's go away. Just for some part of that time. Let's make believe I'm just a college freshman on break and his dad's taken him on vacation.''

Sheriff hesitated.

"I'll pay for it," Roger said desperately.

Michael Sheriff laughed aloud. Roger wasn't kidding. It was just one more example of how far off the norm the two of them were. Roger had been drawing a substantial salary from MIS and he could easily afford the expense of a month-long vacation anywhere on the globe.

"Okay, okay," said Roger, "so that was dumb. But, can we?''

"You make believe you're a normal freshman for a couple of weeks, and if you come up with some pretty good normal freshman grades for your courses, I'll make believe I'm a normal father, and I'll take you on some perfectly normal vacation. And if we're lucky, neither one of us will have to kill anybody."

. . . 3

"JESUS, THIS PLACE is incredible."

"Well," said Sheriff, "you wanted some make-believe."

"No problem. It's great."

Michael and Roger sat leaning against the walls at opposite ends of the sauna of their rented cottage.

Cottage wasn't exactly the right word for a structure that cost a million and a half dollars to build and had a forty-foot living room with a hearth big enough to eat breakfast in, seven bedrooms, eight baths, a kitchen that could have fed the entire White House staff, and a state-of-the-art recreation room. But the Middle Eastern sheik who'd had it constructed in the far northern woods of Maine was probably comparing it to his four palaces when he called it a cottage.

The sheik used it once a year, during deer-hunting season, so he'd been happy to lend the place to Sheriff for a couple of weeks. After all, Michael Sheriff had saved the sheik's life.

For a while the two men were silent, slowing their breath and heart rates, feeling the pores of their skin opening up. Now and then Sheriff wiped his brow and flung the sweat at the heated rocks in the trough near the entrance, and the liquid sizzled and steamed.

This place was so far away from anywhere. The Sheriffs had come by snowmobile. No other houses were within five miles at the least, and at this time of year—the week before Christmas—they were empty. Father and son were alone in the small sauna in the corner of a massive house in the center of a large protected piece of property in the midst of a forest populated only by deer and moose. Intrusion was very unlikely.

"You did pretty well out there this afternoon," said Roger at last.

Michael looked over at his son. In the dim light he couldn't quite make out the features on Roger's face, but he heard the smile in his voice. "You making fun of me?"

"You didn't once tell me how I should carry my rifle while we were skiing."

Cross-country skiing, of course, because it might come in useful someday. Sheriff considered downhill skiing a pointless luxury. Only in James Bond films did international agents congregate at the tops of fashionable mountains. But there might be a number of times when he and Roger would find themselves in uneven winter terrain.

Still, on the workout that afternoon, Michael had been careful not to make the trek *too* much of a lesson in nordic warfare.

Roger stretched, and his father heard a grunt of discomfort.

"Stiff?" Michael asked.

"It works different muscles than running," Roger replied ruefully.

"Stay still," his father said, and climbed down from the bench. He went to the other side of the sauna and encircled Roger's left thigh with his two massive hands.

Roger cried out.

"Easy," said Sheriff, beginning to massage the tendons.

Roger groaned. "Man, that feels horrible."

Sheriff didn't even bother to reply. What was good for you didn't always feel good. After he'd worked on that leg a while, he shifted to the right one. He was so atten-

tive to his task that he didn't even realize how long they'd
been inside the sauna till he felt a river of sweat pouring
down his back. Staying in a sauna this hot could be dangerous even for a man in top shape. "Let's call time," he
said.

"Can't you rub my calves, too?"

"I thought it felt horrible."

"Yeah, well, it feels so good when you stop."

Michael laughed and slapped his son's knotted calf.
He worked those over very quickly and so roughly that
Roger screamed out, and even tried to push away his fa-
ther's hands.

"Enough," Michael said, stopping suddenly. "Let's
go."

He opened the door of the sauna and the steam bil-
lowed out into the tiled dressing room.

Roger was still moaning on the high redwood bench.

"Let's go," Michael repeated impatiently.

Roger climbed down and went out of the sauna, turning toward the showers. Michael grabbed him by the
shoulders and turned him in the other direction—around
the corner of the dressing room and to a small door.

"Where does that—" Roger started to ask his father,
but by that time Michael had already pushed the door
open.

"Outside!" croaked Roger.

A strong gust of December wind suddenly blew snow
in through the door and all over Roger.

"You're crazy," he said to his father, but before he'd
gotten those words out of his mouth, Michael Sheriff had
pushed his naked son out into the snow.

For a moment Roger panicked and thought—no, he
knew—that this was going to be some sort of insane survival thing. His father was going to lock him out of the
house overnight, naked, without clothing, without food,
just to make sure he could survive. Well, he wasn't—

But that wasn't what was happening. Michael Sheriff,
too, came out and threw himself into a bank of snow, and

rolled around in it, covering his naked reddened skin with the white stuff.

It was then, just as Roger was thinking that the heat of the sauna had affected his father's brain, that he realized that though he was sitting naked in a snowbank, he didn't feel cold. It was almost like diving in ocean water in a wet suit—you knew the cold was out there, and in a strange way you could feel it, but it wasn't *really* cold. The sauna had done something to protect him against it. He knew it wouldn't last long, so he did what his father was doing—rolled around in the nearly yard-high cover.

Roger and Sheriff stood up, looked at one another, and laughed. Two naked men with bright red skin smeared with large patches of white.

Roger's smile suddenly faded. "It's wearing off," he said.

"Run for it!" said Sheriff.

They raced back for the door into the house.

A few hours later the two men sat in the living room. This far north, and this far east, it got dark early, not much after three o'clock in the afternoon. Roger had laid a fire and lighted it while Sheriff cooked up a couple of steaks. After the day's exertions, the two men virtually inhaled the meat. Now, in the early darkness, Sheriff sat in a chair pulled up near the fire, and Roger sat perched on the edge of the raised brick hearth, now and then poking the fire or tossing in another log.

Sheriff wore wool slacks, a cashmere turtleneck sweater and a pair of heavy woolen boot socks. Roger wore a sweatsuit and identical socks.

"Drink?" Roger asked.

"Sure."

Michael didn't have to tell his son what he wanted. He always had the same thing: unblended Glenfiddich scotch. He drank it neat, no ice, nothing to interfere with the smooth flavor of the whiskey. He would usually make some remark about Roger having a beer with him at this time—but hell, this was their father/son vacation. He didn't object when he saw that Roger had poured himself a glass of the same liquor, because Michael Sheriff knew Roger was imitating him as a compliment.

After delivering the glass to his father, Roger went back to his station at the hearth.

"How are we doing?" Michael asked.

"Okay." More than okay. They were doing fine. They'd been doing fine now for four days. Skiing, snow-shoeing, their minimal routine of exercises inside the house—minimum being a two-and-a-half hour workout. And in all that time, the telephone had not rung, they'd not seen another human being, and they did not even know that a war had broken out in sub-Saharan Africa.

They stared at the flames, hypnotized.

Finally, Roger spoke. "You know, it's time to go into the next stage of the father/son fantasy."

"It's not fantasy. I'm your father. You're my son. Say what you want. What's the next step?"

"The next step is where I ask you for help. Ask you to understand some things. Difficult things."

"Why does that have to wait for a vacation like this?"

"Because now we're not competing."

Michael watched the fire again. Maybe competing was exactly the right word. If not with his son, then he was competing with MIS and the Chairman for his son. Maybe that was why there'd been so much trouble. Maybe he was just one more parent who was afraid to see his offspring go out on his own.

"Okay," Sheriff said at last, "we're not competing. We're a man and his son and we're all alone in the north country. So shoot, anything you want."

"I want to talk about Stasia."

They'd discussed the dead daughter of the Israeli Consul General before, but only in a cool context. Michael had ideas about how Roger must feel. He'd felt that way before—too many times. Women he'd loved had been killed. It didn't get easier, really, but the first time was still the hardest.

"Sometimes I wonder if it will ever stop hurting," Roger said, staring vacantly into the fire. "Then I realize, no, it won't. When the thought comes through it's like a fist in my gut. It will never stop hurting."

The girl had been beautiful—and different from any girl he'd ever known. When they'd met at Breslauer, they didn't know that they were each the offspring of very special fathers. They were just a couple of students at the university. They'd become close, close enough that she had offered him her virginity, a gift he'd accepted without hesitation. They had tried to believe that they were just like any other teenaged couple falling in love, but of course they weren't. They had different perspectives, with different options for their futures, and different dangers assailed them.

The dangers just caught up with Stasia sooner. An assassin, a member of a cult of Middle Eastern fanatics, had murdered her. Shot her dead while she sat at her dressing table not ten feet away from Roger. Roger had gone after the killer. Found him, barely older than himself. And Roger, reaching right for that kernel of barbarity that was inside him, had exacted his revenge for Stasia's death.

"I think I fucked it up," said Roger. He was turned to the fire. The moisture on his face might just have been perspiration because he was sitting so close to the flames. Or it might have been tears. His father couldn't tell.

Sheriff said nothing.

"I think I should have done *something.*"

More silence. Then Sheriff said, "I've read all the reports. I talked to everyone. I know the feeling. The idea that it was you, you were on duty, you were armed, you were supposed to be protecting her. They got her. It's happened to me. I felt the same things."

"Did you? Did you really?" Roger turned and faced his father. Tears, not perspiration.

"Yeah, I did. Those feelings aren't going to go away. I'm sorry. We live a high-risk game. The winnings are high, and the losses are even higher."

Roger turned back to the fire. This was nothing new. "There's something else about it," he said. "Something I don't like."

"Go on."

"I told you about getting those guys on the Common, remember? They were small-time, real small-time. Three jerks who picked on the wrong guy. I guess I just looked like some WASP from the suburbs with a pocketful of cash."

Michael shrugged. Taking out a trio of hoodlums on the Boston Common was, in his mind, the equivalent of picking up a discarded candy wrapper. A civic duty—and one that made the park a nicer place to walk in.

"There have been other times like that," Roger went on. "At least sort of like that. There's a guy who hangs out where I go sometimes to . . ." Roger stumbled.

"Pick up girls?" his father offered.

"Yeah. Well, this guy thought he was cock of the walk. And he came after me, 'cause I was pretty much just standing there, and . . ."

". . . and the girls came after you," Sheriff concluded.

Roger blushed and grinned. "Yeah. Anyway, he came after me, and I tried to warn him. Told him he couldn't match me. But there's no way to say that kind of stuff and not sound like an asshole. He just thought I was handing him some bullshit. So, he made me fight him. I took him out in ten seconds. No, it didn't even take that long."

"You warned him," said Michael. "He started it, you warned him. Your responsibility stops there."

"Yeah, I know that," said Roger. "But both times, it was something else that bothered me. I *liked* it. I mean, I physically *liked* it. I got off on it. It felt like, after all the hours I'd spent training with you and the people the Chairman sends over for special lessons, I was finally doing something. What does that mean? Is that sick? Should I go report myself to Katrina? Am I still trying to make up for Stasia? Am I still going after the guy who shot her?''

Sheriff took a deep breath. "There are two different things. First, there's the fights. I know what you mean. You spend all that time in preparation for something and then it finally happens. It's cathartic. It's incredibly cleansing. Like jumping in the snow after the sauna. After that long buildup, there you are, all tension and adrenalin, and the fight releases it."

"Yeah," said Roger, and then was quiet a bit longer. "I guess that's it. It's sort of like spending a week reading dirty magazines and never being able to jerk off, then *bam* you get the Big O all at once."

Sheriff blinked at the crudeness of the analogy, then he laughed. "Yeah, though I never thought about it quite that way before. But let me warn you, it won't change. Athletes at least have a definite time when they have to be ready. They have a date and place where their skills will be tested. They can psych themselves up for it. We can't, Roger. Even when you start going out on real assignments—*Jesus,*" he said, realizing suddenly that such a time might not be far away. He recovered almost immediately. "Even when you start being sent out on real assignments, most of your time will be spent in waiting. Just waiting. You wait for twenty-three hours and fifty-five minutes, and then in those last five minutes you have to use every skill you've ever learned and if you don't use them right, you're dead. But the problem is, you never know exactly when the alarm is going to ring."

"Why don't we crack? Do people crack? The tension—"

"—is unbearable sometimes," Sheriff said quickly. "I know. That's why Katrina's there, to make sure the springs don't get wound too tight. And you know, of course, that I have to report on her as well. Make sure *her* springs don't get wound too tight.''

"No," said Roger, "I didn't know that." What he did know was that his father had just entrusted him with a secret, and that made him feel very warm inside. "She'd kill us? If the springs started to snap?"

"No," replied his father. "Not unless she absolutely had to. More likely she'd just report to the Chairman. Then we'd be given a very long and very protected vacation."

"Has that ever happened to you?"

"We're on vacation now, Roger."

THE DAYS IN Maine leading up to Christmas went on peaceably. Michael didn't say a word, but Roger, on his own, brought out the Remington .30-.30 rifles the fourth day and they commenced Nordic training in earnest. Dressed in white suits for camouflage, they skiied cross-country, and Michael showed Roger how to use the blinding reflected rays of the sun most effectively.

"The Finns perfected this, along with the saunas. It's how they nearly beat the Russians during their war in 1939. They could move whole armies on skis, everyone wrapped in white, and the Russians would constantly be picked off. They couldn't get the upper hand on the much weaker Finns until the Baltic froze in a freak cold snap. Then the Russians were able to move their tanks right over the ice. If that hadn't happened, the Finns just might have won."

The exercise with the rifles was grueling. Roger soon understood why this combination of cross-country skiing and marksmanship qualified as an Olympic sport under the name Nordic Biathalon. Few other athletic events combined a struggle with one's body and shooting skills. They would ski at top speed for a period of time and then, on Michael's sudden command, drop to their bellies, aim and fire at a target that Sheriff designated. Then, on to the next stage.

The crisp winter air and the good companionship kept the days moving. The time spent with one another didn't need constant talking to smooth things over, or repetitive expressions of good will to convince them that they were happy to be with one another.

Roger was into it, he realized. He had moved beyond the point where exercise was painful or laborious—it was just what a young man did with his body. He pushed it, he flexed it, not with sideshows for girls or other guys, no ostentatious pumping up of his biceps. No, his body was a machine and all the training that had gone into it was to produce this final result: a physique that could be used.

That didn't mean that he was superhuman. Sometimes he thought that Michael was. Even though they were not in any of their competitive modes, Michael would unconsciously go further, and he'd want and expect Roger to join him. There was always another hill to climb beyond the one they'd just struggled up, or they could always move a little faster, or they could sleep a couple of hours less. There was always something *beyond*, and it always left Roger exhausted.

On Christmas Eve they came back to the house just as a new storm was blowing in from Quebec. The frigid snowy wind pressed at Roger's back, pushing him toward the door of the house. All he could think about was a place that was sheltered with walls, blessed with central heating and clean sheets and a little indoor plumbing. But his father wandered off the drifted path up to the house, calling out, ''Wait!''

Roger waited, without enthusiasm. He felt he could sleep till New Year's.

Sheriff wandered off a few dozen yards, striding through the snow with his axe raised. He looked about for a moment, then bent down, plowed out a bowl in the snow, and chopped at a small pine with his axe.

Then he raised the tiny tree aloft with a smile.

''Tomorrow is Christmas!''

Roger groaned and stumbled inside the house.

It was the smell of cooking steak that wakened him several hours later. He was almost as hungry now as he had been sleepy before. He'd devoured the meat before he was even well awake, and said ruefully to his father, "I don't even remember what that tasted like."

"It's okay," said Sheriff, grinning. "I'll grill you another." And he did.

Sheriff had constructed a small stand for the Christmas tree, and it stood forlorn and naked at the end of the long dining room table.

"It needs something," said Roger, pointing with his fork.

"I hate all that decoration shit," said Sheriff.

"What it needs," said Roger, "is presents."

"Those I brought," Michael replied.

His son blushed. "Me, too."

After they'd cleared the dishes, Michael went upstairs to the bedroom and brought down the gifts he'd hidden in one of his bags. Roger followed after a few moments, and opened *his* bag as well. Down at the bottom Roger came up with two small packages he hadn't seen before. He held them up. "Did you put these in here?"

Sheriff shook his head, and then laughed. "Katrina."

They came down with an armload of gifts each, and spread them out under the tiny bare tree.

"Christmas was always your favorite day," said Michael Sheriff, looking at his son and marveling—not for the first time—that the boy he remembered so well in a crib was now almost six feet tall. "Christmas was just about your first word, as I remember."

"Let's open the presents now," said Roger, with a gleam in his eye.

"You don't grow up, do you?"

"Not about Christmas I don't."

"If we open the presents tonight," said Sheriff, "there won't be any surprises tomorrow." Then he laughed, "I seem to remember making that little speech before. When you were five years old."

"Well, now I'm old enough to vote, and I vote we open our presents."

"Pour us a drink, kid, and we'll see what Santa brought."

Santa brought Michael Sheriff sweaters and watches. Sweaters of cashmere, sweaters of soft sporty cotton, sweaters of precipitation-shedding Icelandic wool. These were from Roger, and the only thing he could think of that he was sure his father would want and wear. He'd actually bought a five-hundred-dollar Italian sweater in the exclusive men's store, Louis, in Boston, and had debated whether to leave the price tag on. At the end he did, but either his father didn't see it, or pretended not to and Roger was disappointed. The watches were from old and grateful clients of MIS who, each Christmas, continued to remember the man who'd saved their lives, their nations, and their fortunes. This year he ended up with an antique Swiss chronograph and two gold Rolexes. He tossed one of the Rolexes to Roger.

"Dad," said Roger in awe, pulling the watch onto his wrist, "are you sure you want to do this? I mean, this baby is worth ten grand or something. Unless it's a knock-off."

"MIS clients don't give knock-offs for Christmas presents, Roger."

"But are you sure—"

"I've got a drawerful of these things at home. There are times I just wish these people would sign me up for Fruit-of-the-Month or something."

Roger mostly received sweaters and shoes. But he also found two sets of long underwear made of dark blue silk.

"Silk?" he asked.

"I'm wearing it now," said Sheriff. "*Very* warm."

Also for Roger was a state-of-the-art portable radio, which wasn't much more than a thin wire with earplugs.

"Who is that from?" Sheriff asked.

"Me . . ." Roger grinned.

Sheriff reached across the table and pulled it off his

son's head. He snapped it apart, and tossed the pieces onto the pile of wrapping, ribbon, and tissue paper on the floor.

Roger started to protest, but Michael cut him off. "Hey, kid, let me tell you something. Your whole goddamn life from now till the day you die is going to depend on the full operation of your five senses. You think I'm going to let you go jogging with that thing on your head? You wear something like that and some guy could get within three feet of you and you wouldn't know it."

Roger thought for a moment before arguing—loud protest had been his initial impulse, because, *goddamn*, that piece of wire had set him back two hundred fucking dollars—but then he saw that his father was right.

The lesson on this vacation was crystal clear: *It's not a game.*

Then Roger, working hard against his inclination, swallowed his harsh words and his anger, and he asked, "I don't see anything from the Chairman. Maybe he doesn't give—"

"This vacation," said Sheriff. "You and me allowed to get off on practically no notice, without Katrina, without any surveillance that I've been able to find—"

"Oh," said Roger quietly. "I hadn't understood that."

"There'll probably be something waiting for us when we get back to the farm."

"What did he give you last year?" Roger asked curiously.

"I got a Christmas bonus last year . . ."

"How much?" Roger asked quickly.

Sheriff paused a moment before replying, "A quarter of a million . . ."

Roger pushed slowly against the back of his chair, but said nothing.

Toward the end of the unwrapping, Roger pulled one package from beneath the small tree that was unlike the others. It was sloppily wrapped in brown paper collected from grocery bags. Roger glanced at his father questioningly.

"It came in the mail just before we left," Michael said noncommittally.

Roger looked at the tag and recognized his mother's handwriting.

A hard expression came over his face, and he tore off the wrapping. Beneath was a cardboard box secured with adhesive tape. He slit the tape and lifted the flaps.

Inside was a small collection of Nevada memorabilia. A selection of shirts from the University of Nevada-Reno. A drinking mug from his old high school. And a couple of joke gifts: canned Sierra Nevada air, a container of water from Lake Tahoe.

He held up a T-shirt advertising the wild west wonders of Carson City and asked his father, "Why is she sending me *junk?*"

"She wants you to come back to her," Michael said quietly. "She thinks they'll remind you of home."

"They do remind me of home," Roger replied with spite. "They're part of the reason I left. I was always up to my ass in shit like this." He got up and flung the T-shirt into the fireplace.

Michael Sheriff was silent till his son got back to the table. "Did you send your mother a Christmas present?"

Roger blushed. "No, I—"

"Don't say you forgot," said Michael.

Roger shook his head. "No, I didn't forget. I just didn't want to."

"I sent something in your name."

"Christ," said Roger excitedly, "I hope you didn't send anything expensive. If that bitch finds out that *I've* got money too, she'll be all over us."

Sheriff looked at his son with stern eyes. "Never, ever let me hear you refer to your mother in that way."

"But she is a b—"

"Roger!"

Roger was silent. He cleared away the wrapping, and at the same time disposed of all the shoddy items that had arrived in the package postmarked Reno.

The two identical small packages from Katrina were all that remained. Father and son opened them at the same time. Inside each package were ski masks, one black and one white for each of the men.

"She think we're going to start robbing banks or something?" Roger asked, disappointed.

"She knitted these herself. The white one's for snow country—camouflage. The black one's lightweight, for disguise—just in case we're ever assigned to rob a bank." Sheriff grinned, and pulled the black mask over his head.

The effect was immediately harrowing—Michael Sheriff suddenly lost all his *bonhomie,* his identity as Roger's father. He sat there, a glowering black totem with an unfeatured visage, two sharply blue eyes peering out intensely.

Roger pulled his white mask over his head, and the effect was the same. For a few moments, the two men stared at one another across the table, faceless, still.

At that moment they heard a small indistinct clattering—like a typewriter—from one of the rooms upstairs.

Roger turned his head sharply.

Sheriff held up a calming hand, rose from the table, and went upstairs.

He came down again a few minutes later, still wearing the mask. Roger still had his on, too.

"Just as well we opened the presents tonight," said Michael, and Roger detected bitterness in his father's voice. "That was a message from the Chairman."

Roger pulled off his mask and flung it aside. MIS again. Just when he and his father had been getting along so well—better than they had at any time since his arrival—his father was going to be sent off to some godforsaken jerkwater country the size of a city block where the natives were blowing up each other with home-made hand grenades.

. . . 5

ON THE DAY AFTER Christmas, the drab, featureless corridor of Management Information Services still bore silver garlands, and small wreaths remained on many of the unnumbered doors. Here and there little strips of discarded tinsel had been caught in the sound-deadening carpet, and the small Christmas tree still stood on the desk of the guard at the subterranean entrance.

The Chairman's secretary, a sweet-faced old woman who looked like the ultimate apple-pie grandmom but who carried a .45 magnum in her purse, was wearing a corsage of holly and mistletoe. She smiled at Michael Sheriff and said, ''They're waiting.''

Sheriff opened the double doors and went into the office of the Chairman of MIS. It was a sensation that was at once exhilarating and daunting, for the only time he came into this large square room was at the outset of a new mission. It was here that Sheriff came to be introduced to the principals of the job—the men who were forced by circumstance to come to MIS as a last resort, men who were willing to pay anything to get the job done. So, each time Michael Sheriff entered this room, he was excited by the prospect of more work, new work, different work in a different place, exercising his manifold skills in a combination that had never presented itself before. But the entrance was also daunting, for he knew that whatever problem these men—and sometimes women—presented to MIS would be the overriding object of all his thoughts and actions for the next several months. He would be wrenched from home, from comfort, and now from family, to be flung into a maelstrom of treachery, danger, and hardship. That apprehension did not lessen with experience; it grew stronger.

The Chairman's office had only narrow slit windows—like those in castles—looking out into the deciduous New England forest surrounding the Fortress. But a large skylight above flooded the room with the diffused light of a gray, lowering day. The office was heavily paneled with mahogany and gumwood, and the few pieces of massive furniture were museum-quality, the best examples of eighteenth-century American craftsmanship. There was no evidence of the mechanical gadgetry that some executives set up in their offices just to show their sympathy with the computer age. The only gadget the Chairman possessed was a single black telephone on the corner of his desk.

In addition to the Chairman, ensconced in a large leather chair behind his desk—the chair didn't even swivel—there were two men in the office. One, obviously an American, was bland and middle-aged. He wore a conservative three-piece suit, white shirt, and striped silk tie.

The other was a foreigner: small, dark-skinned, with bright black intelligent eyes, and a smile that was genuine and irrepressible. He also wore a three-piece suit, and wore it with comfort—which led Sheriff to think him a diplomat, or even perhaps the leader of a small eastern hemisphere nation. Judging by the skin, southeast Asia, probably. And the nation, whatever it was, had to be *very* small, because diplomats and leaders of even marginally important countries quickly had all spontaneity sapped out of them. A representative of the Philippines or Indonesia or even Sri Lanka couldn't have a smile that was as genuine as this man's.

Before he was even introduced, just looking at the two men, Sheriff knew what the situation was. Small country in some sort of trouble, and the small dark-skinned man is here to give evidence and explain exactly what the trouble is. Down beneath the ready smile, he's worried, Sheriff thought. And the other one, the American, is State Department—no, probably American Big Business, with assets in the small country endangered by whatever trouble is besetting the place. The American is unhappy because it is he who will end up paying MIS's fee, and the American is one of those men who want quality, but don't like to have to pay for it.

All this went through Sheriff's mind in the few steps from the door of the office to the desk.

He shook hands with the foreigner. "Mr. Tufalo," said the Chairman, "this is Mr. Sheriff. Mr. Sheriff, Mr. Tufalo is the Ambassador to the U.N. from the Republic of Suparta."

Right on two counts: a diplomat, and from a tiny Pacific island nation.

He shook hands with the American. "This is Mr. Leyland," said the Chairman. "Mr. Leyland is CEO for International Multi-Development Corporation. IMDC has major interests in the South Pacific."

Right on all counts.

The American, Leyland, was pompous to boot. He'd obviously developed a long, rolling, low-pitched voice to deal with stockholders, and he was using that voice to address Sheriff and the Chairman now:

"As you probably already know, we are a high-tech corporation, with headquarters in Wilmington, and major interests in the South Pacific. We have consistently deployed our financial resources, to the benefit of such small nations as the Republic of Suparta, through the development of a technologically sophisticated labor force."

"Cheap foreign labor," the Chairman translated.

The Supartan ambassador giggled.

IMDC's chief executive officer frowned.

The Chairman took over with an analysis that was more to the point: "Suparta was colonized by the Dutch in the eighteenth century, and eventually became a secondary port on the spice lanes. For some reason the natives of the country took to colonialism, were Christianized, and went after education the way that some people"—the Chairman glanced at Leyland—"go after the maximization of profit potential. The first Western-style university in that part of the world was set up in the capital, Satuka, in 1853, and has been in operation ever since. The colony received its independence in 1937, was briefly occupied by Japan during World War II, and then, during the 1950s, received the first major influx of development capital through multinational corporations."

"IMDC was the first," Leyland said gravely.

"And you were there with the most," the Chairman added dryly.

"Considering the size of the fee you intend to extract from us," Leyland said hotly, "I think you might afford us—"

"—a little respect?" the Chairman finished.

Sheriff glanced at Tufalo, and the little man smiled and winked.

"What is the problem in Suparta?" Sheriff asked suddenly.

Leyland was hot and disgusted and wouldn't reply, so Tufalo spoke, easily, charmingly. "In the past year and a half there have been many raids—very destructive raids —on the facilities maintained by IMDC and other companies as well. Bombings, burnings, loss of life—very disturbing incidents on an island as small as ours. We have no history of this sort of violence. Even the Japanese during the war—"

"The Japanese are back." Leyland snorted.

"But not as enemies to the people of Suparta," the Chairman objected, "merely as competitors to IMDC.

Or do you own Japan now?'' The Chairman turned to Leyland. ''I forget.''

''Has anyone claimed responsibility?'' asked Sheriff.

''Religious fanatics,'' growled Leyland.

''Primitive totems of our people have been found in the ruins,'' Tufalo admitted. ''But, of course, anyone with knowledge of our people would know of these primitive gods. And in Suparta the statues are sold to tourists as curios.''

''Who do *you* think is responsible?'' Sheriff asked Tufalo, pointedly ignoring Leyland.

Tufalo shrugged.

''Suparta has importance beyond its ability to supply cheap labor to produce Mr. Leyland's chip-boards,'' said the Chairman. ''The island lies in a section of the Pacific that is perfect for the tracking of satellites, and because of the proven long-term stability of the island, four nations have set up space-tracking and space-research facilities there—the United States, New Zealand, Japan, and the European Space Agency. These stations have not only scientific but military importance, do they not, Mr. Leyland?''

Leyland shifted uncomfortably in his chair.

''We needn't feel very sorry for Mr. Leyland,'' said the Chairman. ''I think if we delved not very deeply into the books of International Multi-Development Corporation we would find that the company expects to be reimbursed by the Pentagon and the CIA'' Leyland started to protest, but the Chairman raised a hand. ''You needn't bother to swear us to secrecy *here,* Mr. Leyland. I've been following the government's attempts to get to the bottom of this. Their not-very-successful attempts. And I'm sure that Mr. Tufalo knows of them as well.''

''Oh, yes.'' Mr. Tufalo smiled.

''So, Mr. Leyland,'' said the Chairman, ''you may tell your backers in Arlington and McLean that Mr. Sheriff will do what he can.''

"This one guy?" sputtered Leyland. "I'm paying fifteen million dollars for one fucking man?"

"Oh, no," the Chairman reassured. "For a mission as important as this, we're assigning Mr. Sheriff a helper."

6

"WHAT *helper?*" Michael Sheriff demanded as soon as Tufalo and Leyland had left the office.

The Chairman only smiled.

"Was that all bullshit?" Sheriff asked warily. He never knew what the Chairman had up his sleeve. He'd worked for the man for years, and never had succeeded in second-guessing him.

The Chairman turned his head and stared at a section of bookcases on a side wall. "All right, Roger."

The bookcase swung smoothly open, and Roger Sheriff stepped into the room. He grinned sheepishly at his father.

"You two were great," he said. "That man Leyland was a total asshole. I liked the other guy though."

"Is that what *you* really thought," asked the Chairman, "or were you just picking up on my not very well disguised contempt?"

"No," said Roger, "I knew it before anybody said anything. Total asshole."

Michael was just staring at the two men. A terrible idea had just come into his head. So terrible he put it out of his mind for a moment.

"You heard everything?" Michael asked his son.

"Saw it, too. Closed circuit. Hey, it's great in there. Dad, there's even these machines that tell if people are lying or not. They must be wired into these chair arms or something—" He looked to the Chairman for verification. The Chairman smiled and nodded.

"Christ . . ." moaned Sheriff quietly. "Listen," he said to the Chairman, "when you told them I was going to have a 'helper' on this mission—"

He didn't have to finish, because he knew the answer from the smug smile on the Chairman's face. Evidently that was confirmation for Roger as well, for Roger grinned. "Oh great, I was sitting back there hoping . . . but I didn't really . . . hey, I mean . . ."

"No way," said Sheriff.

Roger's face fell, and he was silent. He turned his head abruptly away with a terrific blush apparent on his cheeks.

The Chairman said nothing.

"I'm not taking Roger. I'm not taking anybody."

After a moment, the Chairman said merely, "Roger is in training. He will go to Suparta as an apprentice."

"I'm not a fucking D.I.," said Sheriff. "Roger," he said turning to his son, "wait outside."

Roger stood his ground. The Chairman nodded approval: "Roger is here right now not as your son, but as an MIS agent. That is to say that, like you, he is here at my command and my pleasure."

Sheriff's first impulse was to argue, to come up with a line of defense that began, *But Roger is in school . . .* But he knew that any such argument could be beaten down, and his beginning it would be, in its way, an acknowledgment of defeat. So Sheriff said nothing at all.

The Chairman evidently had banked on some such retort, for when Sheriff was silent, he said, "It's been arranged at Breslauer already. The new semester won't begin until February anyway, and if the two of you aren't back by then, Roger will automatically be enrolled in an 'independent study' in the anthropology department. So Roger, pay attention while you're over there. Take notes, and so forth, because when you get back, there'll be a paper to write."

"Yes sir," said Roger quietly to the Chairman, but his hard eyes were focused on his silent, fuming father.

For a few minutes none of the three men said anything at all. Then the Chairman, in dismissal, merely remarked, "Michael, this is an agency, not a family, matter. You two are scheduled to leave in less than a week. If possible, I'd like to have dinner with you before you go."

"We'll be busy packing," Sheriff said harshly, and stalked out the door.

Roger glanced at the Chairman, and then scurried after his father.

Dinner was a silent, uncomfortable affair, and because it was silent and uncomfortable, it seemed formal. And the formality made it even harder for Roger to talk to his father.

But Roger had to talk to him. This was something that had to be discussed. Especially if they were going out in the field together. Their first mission. Roger saw anger in his father's face. Anger and disappointment. And a refusal to speak to his son.

"This assignment . . . One of us could . . ." He trailed off. His father wouldn't help him. "One of us could die," he finished bravely.

"Right," said Sheriff. "You could die, Roger, because you're not prepared for this mission—whatever kind of mission it turns out to be. And I could die as well, because I'm not going to be protecting just my own ass out there, I'm going to have to be thinking about yours. Yeah, so one or the other of us could die, and maybe both."

Roger looked away. He sipped at the large glass of red wine beside the plate. "I guess this is sort of training under fire."

"I guess this is sort of training through stupidity," his father corrected.

"Goddamn it, Dad, I want to go!"

"You've made that clear," said Sheriff, as he returned to his cutlets.

But Roger wasn't going to let him get away with that. "You knew this was coming," he protested. "You knew it would happen sometime."

"I thought it would happen when both of us were ready for it to happen. That's what I thought."

Roger backed down. "I like . . . I like being with you."

"Yeah."

"I hated it when you went away and left me here alone."

Sheriff looked up and looked at his son. He chewed his veal.

"See," said Roger, "I think I know what it is."

"What what is?"

"I think I know why you don't want me along. Because you're jealous."

Sheriff's eyes widened, but he said nothing.

"I think you're jealous that someone might cut in on all the shit you've been getting."

Sheriff put down his fork. "What shit I've been getting?" he echoed.

Roger spread his hands wide. "This house, and everything that goes with it and goes in it. The adventure. The *women*. You're just pissed off because you had to work so hard for it, and I'm going to get it when I'm nineteen. That's what's really got you upset. You think I'm going to cramp your style. You think that from now on you're going to get a smaller piece of the pie."

Something else came into his father's eyes then. Concern. Distress. And that puzzled Roger, but he didn't take back what he'd said.

"That's what you think?" Michael asked. "Or did you just say that to make me mad?"

That sounded like a trick question. Roger thought for a moment, then told the truth. "No, that's what I really think."

"You think I do all the things I do so I can live in a house like this? So I can get laid all the time? So I can buy any car I want and pay cash? I mean, is that what you really think?''

"That's part of it, sure," said Roger. "That has to be part of it."

Michael nodded thoughtfully, neither confirming nor denying the accusation. "And is that why you're in it?" Sheriff asked.

"That's part of it," said Roger. "Dad, you don't know what it was like. Nevada. The shit that goes on out there. You don't know how close I came to all that. Jail, and some dumb chick and five kids before I'm twenty-six, and a beer belly before I'm twenty-three. Listen, I didn't even know people lived like this." He vaguely indicated the house. "I didn't know there were things that *mattered.*"

"You mean there are other things to this kind of life, besides the house and the money and the limitless sex."

"Sure," said Roger quietly. "There are other things."

"What other things?"

"Training. Training for something that's worthwhile, that means something. Doing some good in the world, I guess."

Michael thought about this for a moment, and then nodded—with approval—Roger saw with relief.

"Anything else?" his father asked.

"Yeah," said Roger. "Being with you."

Michael Sheriff poured himself another glass of wine, and moved his plate aside. He pushed the bottle down the long table toward his son, and Roger reached out for it as if it had been made of his father's forgiveness instead of mere green glass.

"So let me get this straight," said Michael Sheriff, "you're in this for three reasons: for the money and power it brings you—sex goes under the category of power, I'm assuming. You're in it to do something good in the world. And you're in it to be with me."

"And to become like you," Roger added quickly. "But yeah, that's it."

"And which of those things is most important?"

To be like you, he started to answer, but didn't. Because that would have been a lie. He told the truth. "I don't know. I can't separate them out."

"Fair enough," said Sheriff. "When I was your age, I was in Vietnam. And even when I knew what I was doing, I couldn't have told you why I was doing it."

"Are you angry at me because I like this money and power? Because I do, Dad, I can't help it. I've never had anything like it, I've never seen anything like it, and when I think that it's *me* who's enjoying it, it's like I get a hard-on or something. I can't help it, I really can't."

"No, I'm not angry. But it makes me sad."

"Why?"

"Because I'm thinking of the time when those things won't mean anything to you any more. When they're no longer rewards for the work that you've done. When they don't give you comfort, and don't make you happy. When they're just *there.*"

"Is that what it's like for you?" Roger asked wonderingly.

His father nodded. "And that's what it'll be like for you someday, too."

"Do you forgive me—I mean, there's . . ."

"There's nothing to forgive," Sheriff said abruptly. "We're both employed by the same company. And soon we go out on assignment together. Which means that we have a lot of work to do between then and now. So put down that glass, and let's get started. Katrina said that the background material was delivered about an hour ago."

7

WHAT A FUCKING WAY to spend New Year's Eve!

The Pan Am jet was riding high over the clouds, and beneath them were the vast, boring stretches of the Pacific Ocean. Roger was not thinking of all that water. He was thinking that this would be the first New Year's Eve in five years—since he was *fourteen*—that he hadn't gotten laid. And he was thinking about the cute ass on the stewardess who was showing her teeth in a constant smile as she served champagne to the other first-class passengers.

The plane wasn't full. The Sheriffs had taken advantage of that and had claimed seats on opposite sides of the wide aisle. Later on in the flight they'd be able to stretch out even more comfortably than now. Not that Roger was complaining about the comfort in the upper lounge of the 747. He loved it.

It was only his father's constant barrage of questions that kept Roger from enjoying the pure luxury of the seat—and the utter beauty of the stewardess's body. Roger was damned if he would give in and ask for a respite, though. Not after the big scene back at Sudbury. No way. Roger was not going to admit or show anything but total involvement and concentration on the assignment.

Michael Sheriff was quizzing Roger on the topography of Suparta. *Again.* Roger thought that in the past week he'd learned more about the geography of that godforsaken country than he knew about the plans for the house he lived in.

Suparta was one of the larger islands in the South Pacific. It was, in fact, one of the few that was large enough in size to have established, long ago and well before the age of exploration, an indigenous and stable civilization. Recent discoveries suggested that there had been numerous exchanges between the ancient Supartans and the peoples of America—the Incas almost certainly—and there were some dark similarities with certain rituals and the *imagerie* of the Aztecs.

The importance of the Aztec link came from the understanding it offered concerning the Supartan religious system, a set of complex rituals and a panoply of gods that had little correspondence with the beliefs and practices of other South Pacific islanders. Worship of the sun was the most obvious and least disturbing similarity.

Both Roger and his father had spent hours poring over books on Aztec and other primitive religious practices. When Roger asked why this depth was necessary on an island that had supposedly left such things behind, Sheriff merely replied that a study of the ancient religion of the Supartans was to be their cover.

That field of inquiry held as much interest for Roger as an Episcopal hymnal. He couldn't have cared less. But, unwilling to admit that he was anything less than the perfectly prepared MIS operative, he'd spent the requisite time reading up on the subject and was more than able, he felt, to carry his weight. After all, he'd merely be posing as the professor's research assistant.

Roger had been more interested in the educational and industrial expansion of Suparta. That was a story! The place was unique. The religious institutions of Suparta had led to the early existence of theological schools. And just as a school for Congregational preachers in Cambridge, Massachusetts, evolved into Harvard University, so had an honored institution of training for sun-worshipping priests served as the foundation for what would become the University of Suparta.

There had been missionaries, of course. Not just Christians from Europe and America, but also Japanese Shintos and Buddhists and even Islamic missionaries as well. Suparta had become a multicultural enclave, its traders bringing with them a host of views that somehow were not only tolerated, but became incorporated into the fluid culture of the island.

It was the missionaries who, once they realized they couldn't dissolve the native religion, decided to turn the small school for priests into a series of colleges, each one at first sponsored by a different religious sect. The sects, in a rare spirit of cooperation, established a secularized undergraduate school to provide basic training for the youth of Suparta. Eventually a medical and nursing school were added, and Suparta now boasted the best hospital between Australia and mainland Asia.

And suddenly Suparta had a university that was recognized as one of the most important in the entire Third World. Just as the great learning institutions of Boston and Cambridge had been directly responsible for the industries that would eventually be clustered around the arc of Route 128, so did the existence of the largest pool of college-educated people in Southeast Asia attract investment to Suparta.

It wasn't that the country was about to become another economic miracle, the way Japan had, but it certainly wasn't the backwater that so many other island nations were, nor was it mired in poverty like most of the rest of the Third World.

The climate was wonderful, a near constant seventy-five degrees Fahrenheit according to the guidebooks, disrupted in only a few months by monsoons. Often the monsoons bypassed the island altogether. The agriculture was sufficient for the island's population. Fruits and vegetables grew in riotous abundance, and the local diet was supplemented with pig, fowl, and fish. There had even been small deposits of a few ores, discovered late in the last century, but the mines quickly ran out. By then, though, they'd provided the endowment for the university and paid for improvements to the port at the city of Pato Lako—improvements enough so the largest cruise ships with their free-spending passengers could find the place an easy stopover.

The pieces had just fallen together for Suparta. It was the size of Connecticut, no bigger. Most of its population of a million or so lived on the island's coast; the central portion of the island remained tropical wilderness. The island's government was a democracy with a figurehead king, descended of a lineage that was now in its thirty-seventh generation of rulers. The king's formal title was perhaps best translated as "Mr. Highness."

When the space above the earth started to become crowded with intelligence and communication satellites, someone noticed that Suparta—always outside the regular Pacific shipping lanes—was in a location ideally suited for the tracking of this extraterrestrial machinery. One by one, the powers-that-be came to Suparta and asked to lease a little wilderness land in order to set up a tracking station. They offered generous terms, and Suparta graciously permitted the stations to be established. All the money received in this fashion was shoveled into the university, which set up a new program in astronomy and celestial studies. The island had come full circle: Its inhabitants once again worshipped the sun.

The four tracking stations, with their tens of millions of dollars worth of equipment, were located deep in the forests of the western portion of the island. Pato Lako, the largest city on the island, lay on the southeastern coast. The capital and home of the university, Satuka, lay on the northeastern coast. After those two, the largest town was a single-hotel resort on the northern coast; nothing else was bigger than a village.

Roger had a pretty good idea of the history and current situation of the island, and he knew what it looked like.

The research division of the Fortress had come through with video tapes, news clippings, audio tapes of religious rites, and binder after binder of photographs and dossiers. Roger had had to study the university catalog as if he were preparing for an undergraduate career there. But his father warned him that this was, after all, just background information. They needed to fully comprehend, Suparta, and the understanding had to be working knowledge; on missions he didn't so much need facts as *understanding* of facts.

"And what they never tell you," Michael added, "is how a place smells."

"Huh?" Roger asked.

Sheriff just laughed.

Roger still didn't quite understand what his father meant, but he knew it was part of the reason Katrina had prepared food that simulated the diet available on the island in the week before they left. Everything tasted as if it had been dipped in melted peanut butter—the morsels of pork and chicken and the varied and plentiful vegetables. It staggered him to think how much it must have cost MIS to transport a week's worth of breadfruit to Sudbury, Massachusetts, in midwinter. But it was a staggering that Roger enjoyed. He loved the evidence of the value the corporation put on him and his father—Management Information Services spared no expense in the training of its operatives.

It was one of Roger's favorite phrases, and it played over and over in his mind. *Spared no expense.*

Roger was pretty sure that this trip to Suparta was going to be an easy exercise. He could even imagine that the whole thing was no more than a training mission, fabricated and set up by the Chairman. Maybe his father was even playing a part. Well, Roger would keep his eyes open, and he'd do good work. That's all there was to it.

8

ROGER WOKE with a start. His shorts felt so damp he wondered if he'd come in his sleep. He'd been dreaming of the Supartan women he'd seen in the videotapes supplied by MIS—bare-breasted and performing swaying native dances. Wide hips were a mark of attractiveness in Supartan women, and Roger liked wide hips.

He shifted in the seat. Nope. He hadn't ejaculated. It was just sweat.

He looked out the window and saw the surf and beach below. The 747 was rapidly approaching Honolulu airport. His father was across the aisle, awake and gauging the landing. Roger checked his seatbelt to make sure it was fastened, then allowed himself another yawn. They'd have an hour here, then take a connecting flight for Suparta.

The giant plane touched the runway and the engines roared as they were reversed to brake the craft. The too-well-rehearsed voice of the chief stewardess came over the loudspeaker.

"Ladies and gentlemen, we request that you remain seated until the plane has come to a complete stop at the terminal. At that time . . ."

Roger tuned out.

In a matter of minutes they were at the gate. Roger was disappointed that the airport in Honolulu was so similar to the one they'd left in Boston, and the one they'd changed in at Los Angeles. More flowers, and it seemed warmer, but that was about the only difference.

"Let's have a cup of coffee," Michael suggested.

"Maybe a drink . . ."

"Roger, you guzzled champagne on that flight for as long as you were awake. Look at your watch. It's seven o'clock in the morning. We are *not* having a drink."

Roger acquiesced and followed his father into a coffee shop. They sat, and even before they were served, his father opened and began to read the local paper he'd just bought at a newsstand.

If there's any more excitement on this trip, Roger thought, *I'm going to have a heart attack.*

Half an hour before departure time of the plane to Suparta, Roger and his father made their way through the security checkpoint.

Roger's sense of time was confused. It was eight o'clock in the morning by Hawaiian time, which meant it was—what?—eleven o'clock, or even noon, by Los Angeles time, which meant it was three o'clock in the afternoon in Boston. But he still felt groggy and disoriented, as if he'd been on a plane since July.

But however early it was in Roger's mind, it was prime time in his loins. The airport was full of beautiful stewardesses, many of them exotic Asians. He heard languages he couldn't even identify in the corridors of the airport. All of these different women with their lovely lilting voices and their fine firm bodies, tight asses and high breasts.

It was one of the problems of traveling with your father. How could you pick up a woman with your old man standing right next to you? More realistically, Roger admitted, how could you jerk off with him still in his seat, wondering why you were in the toilet for so long?

Still, it was pretty good, being in Hawaii, traveling first-class, seeing all this skirt, getting—

Roger was suddenly frozen with shock. For one moment he had simply been walking alongside his father,

just like the tourists in front of them and the tourists behind them, when all at once Michael Sheriff bolted
through the security check, scattering guards and passengers alike. He threw himself onto the back of the man
who had just passed through, a man in a good-looking
but ill-fitting three-piece suit. Just a normal businessman, and there was Roger's father right on top of him.

The security guards at the metal detectors reacted first,
pulling their weapons.

Oh shit, Roger thought, *he's going to get killed by
these bozos.*

The two men were fighting, and all the tourists were
screaming. Roger fought to get through the passengers
who were all trying to go the other way.

There was one shrieking scream, louder than the
others, as Michael found a hold on his opponent and
threw him over his shoulder. The guy slammed into one
of the shatterproof windows of the concourse. As promised, the glass didn't break, but the force of the man's
flight made it crack into a pattern like a spider's web. The
center of the web was the man's head.

The corpse's head, Roger realized.

It had to be a corpse. The back of the skull had cracked
open when the man made contact with the glass. Roger
could tell, because as the dead man slowly slid down the
glass he left behind a trail composed of more than blood.
There were those gray lumps of ooze, stuff that Roger
knew was brain cells—this guy's memory of his mother
or something like that—and it was now smearing over the
window. When your memory of your mother seeped out
of your skull, it meant that you weren't going to remember *anything* anymore.

Michael Sheriff was panting. He rubbed his hands on
his good linen slacks, the ones they had bought at Brooks
Brothers in the tropical clothing department. He looked
up, and frowned at Roger's puzzled expression. That
seemed to bother him more than the security guards' guns
that were pointing at him.

"Open his coat," said Sheriff.

Something in his matter-of-fact tone was persuasive. One of the guards went over and folded back the dead man's jacket. A slew of plastic weapons spilled out—knives that had not shown up on the metal-detecting machines.

"Other side, too," said Sheriff.

The security guard reached in gingerly and pulled out a flattened packet of material—gelatin, Roger realized.

The security guards saw that, too, and Michael Sheriff didn't have to explain that he'd just stopped a man armed with plastique explosives from getting on a plane.

Stopped him good.

They might have missed their plane out of Honolulu, but the airport authorities kept the Air Suparta machine on the ground for an extra ten minutes just for Roger and Michael's sakes. The Air Suparta was not as big as a 747, but it was big enough for first-class comfort again.

They took their reserved seats and buckled their belts. "Was he after this plane?" Those were actually the first words that Roger had spoken to his father since the incident. There hadn't been time or the opportunity at the airport. The police and federal authorities came in droves as soon as it was reported that a civilian had taken out a would-be hijacker who'd passed through airport security. Michael was taken into temporary custody, but hurried telephone calls to military headquarters in Honolulu, to Washington, and to MIS headquarters, assured Michael's release.

The Hawaiian police had at first been insistent—they had to have Michael for questioning. In their minds it was impossible that he had no foreknowledge of the incident. At the very least—

But one particular telephone call from Washington had caused the head of airport security to announce that cer-

tain new facts had come to his attention. This distin-
guished scholar from Massachusetts had actually had
nothing to do with the incident. He'd merely been a by-
stander, as frightened as any other. It was an undercover
security agent who spotted the terrorist—now identified
as a member of a rabid international cell—confronted
him, fought with him, and killed him.

They were all very sorry that Mr. Sheriff and his assistant had been inconvenienced. Of course, please, call Air
Suparta and make sure that the two men weren't going to
miss their plane. So sorry again, our apologies. They
seemed as anxious now to have Sheriff on his way as before they had been insistent on detaining him.

"Was he after this plane?" Roger repeated. He wasn't
worried about any sweat in his crotch now; he was more
aware of the cold clammy feeling that was like acid in his
armpits.

"No." That's all Michael would offer. He seemed angry.

"What? Come on, please, what?"

"You didn't notice, did you? What was the matter,
Roger? Too busy drooling over stewardesses to pay attention to the world around you? You're an MIS operative in the field, kiddo. A pro—supposedly. You're
expected to be paying attention to *business*, not chasing
pussy like a teenager."

"I *am* a teenager," Roger protested weakly.

"The whole point of your coming on this goddamn
mission was that you promised you wouldn't *act* like
one."

Bastard, thought Roger. But his anger was directed at
himself. They weren't even halfway to Suparta, and he'd
just had Strike One. He hadn't even seen the ball coming.
Hell, he hadn't even known the pitcher was on the
mound.

The plane began to taxi down the field.

Okay, fix it, Roger thought. Figure out where you

went wrong. Find the pieces that, put together, had prompted his father to attack.

Roger closed his eyes and played the scene in his mind.

They were walking down the corridor. Okay. There was a crowd. No big deal, a crowded airport. He remembered seeing the man walk through the little archway of the metal detector. The alarm went off. Right, the alarm had gone off, but it couldn't have been plastique that did it. What? Change and keys. Like so many people, the guy had accumulated so many small pieces of metal in his pockets that the alarm had been set off.

Even Roger's peripheral vision was working in his memory, like a videotape in which everything is in focus. He remembered the particularly attractive Malayan women who were coming toward him. He'd wondered if the smiles on their faces were for him, or for his father, or for both.

But then the man in front of them had placed all his stuff in one of those plastic containers. Walked around the archway and then back through again, and this time the alarm *didn't* go off.

On the other side, the guard checked him with the hand-held metal detector. He stood there, like Napoleon, with his right hand over his breast.

"His hand," Roger said aloud. "When the guard put the detector on him he covered the plastiques with his right hand."

Sheriff looked up from his magazine.

"Right. First clue."

The plane was gaining altitude. Roger went back to the scene in the airport. "Then he smiled. A weird smile."

"Why?" asked Sheriff, putting down the magazine. He no longer sounded quite so angry.

Roger searched for an answer. "He was nervous? He thought he had gotten away with it?"

"Two down," said Sheriff.

"That's not enough to give him away though," said Roger. "Everybody is nervous about metal detectors. But then you hit him. What was the other clue?"

"His suit," said Sheriff.

"It was expensive," said Roger. "And it didn't fit."

"No, it fit. He just didn't know how to wear it. He was trying to look like a businessman, but he didn't know how to wear a three-piece suit."

Roger nodded. "Anything else I missed?"

"The point of a dagger, sticking out of his shirt cuff. It only showed when he dropped his change in the plastic cup."

"Jesus," said Roger, "you do see everything."

"Well," said Sheriff, "I have to admit, I had one advantage over you: I recognized his face from an Interpol flyer," Sheriff admitted. "He was a—what?—an associate member, I guess you'd say, of the Baader-Meinhof gang. Assumed to be living in Libya."

"I couldn't have known that. That—"

"You're right," Sheriff agreed. "I saw that flyer years ago."

"And you remembered?"

His father nodded.

Suddenly something else occurred to Roger. "Why did you attack him that way? You actually fought with him—why? You were after something *on* him, weren't you?"

"The pull string in his other cuff," Sheriff said approvingly. "The one that would have detonated the plastique. He was a true believer. The kind who wouldn't have minded going if he could take a couple of dozen tourists and guards with him."

"Where was he going?" Roger still wanted to know.

"He was picking up the plane we came in on, on its continuation flight to Tokyo. There's a delegation of South Korean diplomats who've been in Hawaii for a major—supposedly secret—negotiation with the U.S. Remember a couple of years ago when some terrorists

managed to kill off half the Korean cabinet in a suicide
raid in Burma? This guy thought he'd do the job on the
other half. He nearly did.''

"If it hadn't been for you—"

"If it hadn't been for my training," Sheriff corrected.

9

THEY CLEARED customs at the airport at Pato Lako without problem. As they walked through the terminal, it was Michael Sheriff's turn to seem as nonchalant as Roger had been in Honolulu. Roger knew what that meant—it meant that his father trusted *him* to be on guard against possible danger.

Roger looked into every face, and scrutinized every sudden movement.

"Ease up," said Michael casually. "You're acting like a bodyguard."

Roger relaxed a little.

There were women here, too, beautiful women. Their breasts were covered. Roger knew he should have expected that—this was, after all, an international airport, and you couldn't expect to have tits exposed over the computer terminals. But Roger still couldn't get those videotapes out of his mind.

Hell, if he could see in the flesh just *half* of what his fantasy had painted for him—

"Those two," he said suddenly, without knowing he had said it, without knowing exactly what made him say it.

The two men by the front door. One of them almost certainly American, one of them maybe American, maybe not. One of them a little older than his father, the other a little younger. They looked out of place here, too well dressed. It looked as if they'd had their hair razor cut in Manhattan that morning. The way they stood, the way—

"Good," Sheriff said approvingly, as he walked straight up to them.

Roger tried to repress the grin that came over him. So he *had* got it right. Maybe those two hadn't been out to kill them, but they had been waiting for them. Roger followed his father.

Before Sheriff reached the two men, they turned sharply on their heels and went out the front door of the airport.

Sheriff and Roger followed. A blast of moist tropical air nearly knocked Roger down. A quality of air, and a range of odors that he'd never before experienced. Too, they were below the equator, and even the goddamn *sun* looked and felt different. Suddenly he understood what his father had meant about MIS's background information never telling you what a place smelled like.

The four of them stood together, off to the side a little, in the shade of a concrete overhang. The concrete seemed to radiate the tropical heat. The shadows were a deep blue.

"Surprised to see me here?" the older man asked.

"No," said Sheriff. "I'd heard you'd been transferred. Ambassador Barton, this is . . . ." Sheriff paused a moment before he completed the introduction. "This is my assistant Roger," he said.

Maxwell Barton, the ambassador of the United States to Suparta. Roger remembered reading the dossier. The man with him was his chauffeur—and his lover. The lover didn't get introduced, but he looked hard at Roger, and there was a weird, unpleasant smile on his face as he regarded him.

Roger held out his hand to the ambassador. He glanced at it, did not proffer his own, and then looked back to Roger's father.

"You're part of the reason I'm here," he said. "I've got you to thank for sending me to this tropical shithole."

"Don't you like the weather?" Sheriff asked.

"Not particularly. I burn in the sun, you can't swim because of the sharks, and the cockroaches grow to the size of cow turds. I was better off in goddamn India."

"Yes," said Sheriff, "Diplomats like you always thrive better under corrupt governments."

"Listen, you—"

"So what do you want?" Sheriff demanded suddenly, as if the vituperative exchange had suddenly grown boring.

"I just wanted you to know that there's going to be a tail on your ass—and your *assistant's* ass—the whole fucking time you're here. You hot-shot MIS guys think you can outdo the Agency any time you want to rake in a few tens of millions."

Roger looked at this man with amazement. He looked like the president of a suburban garden club; didn't talk like it, though. And just how much did he know? He obviously knew that Sheriff was MIS, and he'd probably realized that Roger was part of the organization, otherwise he'd never say all this within his hearing. He looked around for the other man. He'd gone. Roger hadn't even noticed when he'd left, or what direction he'd gone in. He'd just slipped off. Probably training of some sort.

Roger had heard a little of his father's former encounter with Maxwell Barton. He had been ambassador to India, and had tried to get Sheriff out of there as well. It hadn't worked. Sheriff had humiliated him and his CIA cohorts when, with the help of an obscure religious sect, he'd squelched a fomenting revolution on the Pakistani border.

No wonder Barton was pissed off. He'd changed territories, and here was Michael Sheriff again.

"I'm here doing anthropological research," was all Michael said.

"With your assistant?" he asked caustically, glancing at Roger. It was not a friendly glance that started at his face but dropped down to his crotch. "What sort of anthropological research? Male fertility rites? I'm told that the local circumcision ceremony is a hoot. It's done with the teeth."

Roger blushed.

"Listen, did you come to invite us to dinner at the embassy?" asked Sheriff.

"In a pig's snatch," the ambassador snarled. A stretch black Cadillac had pulled up, and Alex Bollow got out of the front seat. Wordlessly, he came around and opened the rear door for Ambassador Barton.

"Then if you're not going to invite us to dinner, my young friend and I would like to get on to the hotel. We've been on the plane all day."

"Just be careful," said Maxwell Barton. "And remember. Old King Kong lives in that fucking rain forest out there. And he tromps down hard on guys like you. Guys like you—they sometimes get squashed into toe jelly. And their little friends, too."

"It's always pleasant to run into old friends in faraway places, Barton. But for right now, fuck off."

"Something was going on that I didn't like," said Roger, at dinner. The Royal Suparta Hotel had two restaurants, one which gave a semblance of native foods on the menu, and the other whose menu was a bland amalgam of bad French, mediocre Italian, and boring American. Sheriff suggested the latter, not because the food was better, but because there was no nonsense about sitting cross-legged on the floor. "We'll get enough of that when we get into the interior," he said.

Roger was disappointed, because the "native" restaurant had dancing girls.

"What didn't you understand?" Sheriff asked.

"The weird way those men were looking at me," said Roger. "I mean, I don't think they were after my bod—"

"No," his father said dryly, "they thought *I* was."

Roger's mouth dropped open.

Sheriff continued to eat, unperturbed.

"They thought I was *queer?*" Roger cried when he'd regained the power of speech.

Sheriff nodded.

"Why didn't you *say* something? Why'd you let them think—"

"I didn't say anything because it's better if they believe it."

"Why?"

"Because it's false information. And Barton right now is an enemy—no, that's not right. He's a *potential* enemy. And if he thinks that I have a weakness for boys, that's great—because I don't."

"Shit. . . ." Roger breathed huskily.

"Also," Sheriff went on, "because he is homosexual, he might just be a little bit more kindly disposed toward me if he believes that I am, too. Sometimes gays are like that, thinking they belong to some kind of conspiracy. Sometimes they take care of each other."

"But don't you *care?*"

"I don't like him. I don't trust him. He's not on my side. Why should I care what he thinks of me?"

"But . . ."

"What I care about—and what *you* should care about —is getting the job done. Roger—another lesson for you, that you should have learned some time ago: We're not in this business to get a double-page spread in *People* magazine. We're not stopping revolutions so that complete strangers can say nice things about us behind our backs. I didn't break that terrorist's head open in order to impress the porters in the Honolulu airport. You *do* understand that, don't you?"

"Yes," said Roger, half grudgingly.

"The more they know about you," said his father, "the easier it is to get you."

"But now it'll go into the records that you're a fag—"

"I hope it does. And I hope it goes in your file, too."

"Jesus!"

"Don't you realize, Roger, that in a short while—if not already—the KGB, the CIA, and all the other intelligence agencies in the world are going to have a file on you. The one thing they want to know most is the one thing that makes you scared. Rats. Snakes. Heights. Being closed in. Needles. That's what they want to know. And one of the easiest weapons they have, especially against uptight assholes like the CIA clones, is to discover that these men are terrified of being homosexual. You get a man like that, and he tries to go straight, but once in a while he slips up. He fucks some guy. Well, you can bet your ass that the guy who seduces him is on the payroll of the CIA, or the KGB, or whoever. Look, you're totally pissed off right now because this man—whom nobody in his right mind would have one ounce of respect for—you're upset because he thinks you're queer."

"I sure as hell am."

"Then that's a weakness, because you're upset. You're distracted, you get it? Why the hell do you think that college sports coaches are always slapping their players' asses?"

"What's that got to do with anything? Hell, I don't know."

"They have to get those guys used to men touching their asses, and maybe their balls. They can't let a player out on the field scared to death that someone's going to feel him up. All the muscles and all the skill in the world would disappear if they just fell apart just 'cause some guy grazed their crotches. And the other team could use it as a weapon. Now do you see? You can't have that fear inside you."

"I'm not afraid."

Sheriff laughed. "You're scared shitless. But Roger,

let me tell you something. Nobody who hunts down girls the way I've seen you work has any problem in that direction.''

That made Roger feel a little bit better.

10

ROGER SAT AT THE EDGE of the hotel pool and looked list-
lessly about him. They'd booked at the Royal Suparta.
Roger remembered his images of dancing girls, the
naked-breasted women he had watched longingly on the
videotapes.

Not here.

The Royal Suparta was a Best Western resort. The
whole thing was a fake stage-setting as plastic as the
worst Disneyland imitators. It must have been an over-
sight on the part of the planners that the palm trees were
real. Certainly the corporation architect would have pre-
ferred fake ones—because fake ones didn't shed, and
didn't house colonies of annoying insects. The problem
was that, in Suparta, fake trees didn't bend with the
strong winds and they required more upkeep than the real
ones.

And the women?

Tourists. Each and every bikini-clad woman there was
a tourist. The cocktail waitresses were all American and
blond. No naked breasts, no grass skirts. None of it was
real.

And the real problem was, of course, that it wasn't
Roger's fantasy.

Roger studied one woman after the other. They were at
least scantily dressed, though some of them shouldn't
have been. He tried to make the best of his disappointment, and to concentrate on the idea of so many women

71

right about him. He needed to do that. Especially after
what his father had said. That Michael Sheriff didn't care
if the ambassador of the United States to the sovereign
nation of Suparta thought that he and Roger were fags.

Roger felt himself shrink inside his Speedo. There had
to be some limit to what was expected of him by his father and MIS.

Maybe, Roger glowered, it was just another trick of
Michael Sheriff's to get him to quit the company. Oh,
he'd like that all right. He probably had an open return
ticket for Roger in his suitcase, just waiting for Roger to
call it quits. Then Michael could get to play daddy on his
days off with an obedient little son waiting at home for
the occasional in-between-assignment vacations.

Fuck him.

Roger kicked at the water angrily. He was not going to
be talked out of MIS and the career and the money it offered. If his father thought that some series of college
hazing tricks was going to work and get him to chicken
out, then Roger would show him that he did, too, have
the right stuff.

The right stuff was beginning to bulge in his swimsuit.
The tight crotch covering was confining, but there was no
doubt that Roger was feeling just what a man he really
was. Sure as hell! He could prove that to his father as
well. Let Michael Sheriff play mind games with the ambassador. Roger had some games of his own to play.

He took another look at the women at poolside, view-
ing them with a new eye and appreciation. He focused on
a pair of women who sat across from him. Everything
about them screamed *stewardess*. They were rubbing
tanning lotion on one another, slowly, languidly, seductively. If there was any guy at poolside who got off on the
idea of two chicks making it, then that guy had just
creamed in his polyester jeans. Roger smiled to himself.
*Let Dad walk in on me with the two of them in bed and
then he'll see what I'm made of.* He could see himself
sprawled on the clean, crisp sheets, one of the women—

the redhead—straddling his face, the other down between his legs. *Yeah.*

Now the small swimsuit was getting very uncomfortable. So much so that Roger quickly became embarrassed. The thing couldn't hold in his erection if he didn't get these thoughts under control. He leaned forward and dove into the cool water of the pool. His only hope was to ignore the growing bulge, get his mind off the women for a minute. If he was going to make this a full seduction, if he was going to claim a prize tonight that would prove something to himself and his father, he'd have to do it later, when he could have a pair of pants on over his shorts.

Instinctively, Roger began to do laps of the pool. Not the slow and calm movements of the tourists—he was immediately the athlete in training. His arms pounded the water's surface and his legs churned a path.

It was late in the afternoon, and his father—in the guise of Professor Michael Sheriff of Breslauer University— was off at the university presenting his credentials. Most of the hotel crowd was either down at the beach, in their rooms napping, or off on some small excursion arranged by the management. If there had been any number of people in the pool, Roger certainly wouldn't have been able to swim back and forth with such blind, repetitious energy. The simple ticking off of laps became more than that, without Roger's even making a decision to go harder. He'd lost count, and was simply watching his energy level. Feeling it drop, and then pushing it higher. Using up what wasn't there. Siphoning off power from places he didn't know he had power left in.

The best thing about physical exertion, Roger had discovered in Michael's torturous training program, was the way it cleansed your mind, let you go free, allowed you to forget things. And not only things, but allowed you to forget emotions as well. Like the way he'd felt when Maxwell Barton looked at him with such contempt. That's what he wanted now. He wanted to forget his an-

ger toward his father, his embarrassment, his fear that—
after all—he might actually disappoint Michael Sheriff
on this mission. He hadn't allowed himself to think about
that before. Now the thought flitted through his brain and
then his flailing arms churned it away in the water that he
left in his wake. All he could feel was his muscles, the
tightness that was building up inside them as he continued to press.

He was entering that gray zone, the one where endurance takes over and the luxury—or the burden—of emotions is obliterated, when he sensed something. Another
presence beside him. There was someone else swimming
laps in the pool. At first he thought his father must have
come back to join him early. Angry at the intrusion into
what he had thought was going to be his own time, Roger
sped up, ignoring the growing pain in his lungs. But
when the other body was barely able to maintain itself beside him he knew it couldn't have been Michael Sheriff.

Roger kept swimming his laps. One, two, three more.
The body kept pace with him. No more, but not any less
either. The speed of their swimming and the blur of the
water between them kept Roger from seeing just who it
was that was racing him. Then suddenly he felt he had to
know who it was beside him. He stopped in the shallow
end of the pool and stood on the concrete floor. There he
waited while the other figure, not anticipating his stopping, kept on for another full lap.

It was a woman.

That was the first thought that went through Roger's
mind. He could see her bathing cap and the straps of her
bra. She maneuvered her turn deftly against the opposite
wall, returning to his end of the pool with clean, even
strokes. This time when she found the edge of the pool
she too stopped and stood.

Dreams come true sometimes. Roger remembered all
the exotic women he'd seen during their trip here. Now,
in the form of near female perfection, was an Asian
beauty. It was as though someone had taken notes on all

his responses and all his daydreams and had created a living person from his desires. He took in her features and
decided she must be Chinese.

Her chest expanded with the need to get oxygen into
her lungs. He studied the heaving mounds. Fabulous:
large, standing out over the sleek waist and full hips. He
could make out long legs through the water's surface.
She looked great—but her tits! Fabulous. The nubs of her
nipples showed clearly through the stretched Lycra of her
racing swimsuit. They were so obvious to his eyes that he
could just imagine reaching out and taking hold of one of
them between his lips, nibbling.

She broke his concentration by reaching up and pulling
off her cap. An incredible amount of black hair, damp
only at the ends, fell down over her shoulders.

"You're good," she said.

She spoke with no overt emotion. Her appraisal was
like that of a teammate, or an appreciative competitor.
She ran her tongue along her lips to clean off the drops of
pool water that still clung there. For some reason, after
all the attention Roger had given her breasts, that one
small thing really did it to him: the sight of the little pink
tongue moving seductively over her lips.

Then she turned and walked to the small ladder at the
side of the pool. He followed, holding to the sides of the
ladder as she climbed out. Heat surged through his body
as he saw, so closely, her round hips swiveling as she as-
cended. But more erotic by far was the glimpse of pubic
hair that curled out from the tight elastic bands at the apex
of her legs.

At the top of the ladder Roger had to pull on his suit in
the usual macho way, but with the real purpose of
rearranging himself before he pulled off some kind of
kinky sex thing right there at poolside.

"Drink?" she asked.

He nodded. Thank God she didn't ask him if he was
old enough. She turned and he found himself following
her silently. Now, again, he was watching those hips,

frustrated that he wasn't getting that wonderful close-up view she'd flashed while they were on the ladder.

They stopped in front of a pair of lounge chairs. She stopped a waitress and ordered two margaritas. Roger didn't even notice that she hadn't asked for his preference. After the waitress had left with the order, she sat on the lounge chair and pointed to the other for Roger.

Roger dropped down into the chair, and at the same time turned his head toward her. His mind was finally forced to consciousness and was able to make some quick calculations. She was tall, perhaps five-ten. He could see from the firm lines of her thighs that she was used to exercise. It had been no fluke that she was able to keep up with him in the water. She was older than him—she could have been thirty, easily.

In a moment, after thinking through all that, he noticed that she was observing him with the same detachment, making the same judgments about his body. Self-consciously he looked at himself and observed what she was seeing. He had grown some more body hair recently, and the thin but even covering across his chest didn't betray his youth. His stomach was naked of hair, except for a long, thin trail that disappeared into his swimsuit—the same swimsuit that was not successfully covering up how excited she made him. His legs were thick, not kid's legs anymore, not after all the running he'd done back in Massachusetts. His arms, too, he realized, had increased substantially. Not really meaning to, he flexed them just a bit, as though testing the size of his growing biceps.

The drinks arrived. The woman signed the check and handed Roger his cocktail. "Cheers." She lifted her glass.

"Cheers," he responded.

"You can talk."

Roger blushed furiously, just then realizing that the toast was the first word he had spoken. "Yeah, I can talk. No problem with that."

"I'm Lin. Lin Tao."

"Roger Baynter." *Baynter* was his mother's maiden name, and the name that had been assigned to Roger as Professor Michael Sheriff's student assistant.

"Have you been in long?"

"No, not at all. We just arrived today."

" 'We?' " She arched an eyebrow.

"Yes," he said glibly. "I'm here with a professor from school. He needed an assistant to take notes, and I needed an independent study. Great way to spend winter break. It's my senior project," he lied suddenly, hoping she would think him at least a few years older than he was.

"What is your professor studying in Suparta?"

"Religion." He drank his margarita and hoped that this topic of conversation would go away. He didn't want to betray his ignorance, and there were much more interesting things to talk about anyway.

"How interesting," Lin said. "I'd like to hear more about it. I've been here for quite a while, but I know very little about the native culture."

"Well," Roger said uncomfortably, "like I said, we just got here. I've done all the reading, but I'm really just here to take notes and sort of be a packhorse."

"I imagine you'd make a pretty good packhorse. With those shoulders."

Roger grinned into his margarita.

"Do you know enough about the religion of Suparta to discuss it over dinner?"

"Sure," said Roger.

"Tonight?"

Roger nodded.

"Fine. Give me an hour. I know a place where we can watch the sun set. You never saw a sunset till you've seen one in the South Pacific. Suite 1500."

She stood then, smiling down at him. Once more he was at eye-level with those hints of pubic hair, and felt that rush of blood through his system. She walked away without saying anything else.

For a moment Roger was stunned into silence. Then he realized that his fears of exposing himself were becoming real again. He quickly readjusted his suit and wondered where he'd find a pair of loose, baggy trunks for the rest of the trip. This Speedo crap was fine for exercising at home, but it obviously wasn't going to work on vacation with women like Lin Tao around.

11

"ARE YOU ENJOYING yourself?"

"It's like a movie," Roger replied. She probably thought he meant the night's activities. He meant her.

He had dressed casually: just a sports shirt, a tropic-weight jacket and light-colored linen pants. When she'd answered the door of Suite 1500—a *big* suite, he noted—she was wearing a thin cotton dress. Very thin; and there was obviously no bra underneath it. He could see those beautiful nipples again.

She had known a wonderful restaurant near the beach, only a little bit away from the hotel. They'd strolled casually down the road toward the water, and she'd enticed him into an easy and comfortable conversation.

If she had thought him tongue-tied at the hotel, he certainly didn't give her that impression tonight. She wanted to hear everything about him. He was able to see just how well he'd learned his lesson about maintaining a cover. It was easy, really, once you got the hang of it, and he told himself he was using this seduction as a way of practicing his technique.

Just as he had been taught, he kept as close to the truth as he could. There was more than enough meat to his story to make it sound very real. A kid growing up in Nevada with his mother, his divorced father absent, and recalled only in postcards and an occasional visit. Then the father disappeared altogether. The life of the normal American kid.

That father—in this version of the story—was never found. Instead, Roger used his brains and took advantage of some luck and got a scholarship to a big, prestigious university in the East. It was an escape route, a way he could get away from the mediocrity of his life.

It was a great story, he thought. Evidently Lin agreed. She was wrapping her arm around his by the time he'd gotten to the divorce of his parents. When he'd finished with a description of the relief he'd felt on his arrival at Breslauer, she had run a hand across his cheek.

"You must have been a very good student to have made an opportunity like this one. A very, very good student."

He hung his head in mock modesty.

The restaurant was wonderful. They sat on the floor. While the waitresses here didn't have bare breasts either, they were certainly natives, not American exiles like the ones at the Royal Suparta. Everyone ate with the fingers—and the menu was varied: fatty pork and wonderfully spiced rice that was dunked in any number of sauces, presented in a tray with more than a dozen shallow depressions in it.

There was a strange-tasting and—Roger would learn—very potent sugar liquor that went easily down his throat. He loved it, he loved the haunting sounds of the drums played by the native band. Two teenaged girls sat crosslegged before the drums and sang unending, monotonous songs in the native language. But most of all Roger loved this sympathetic Asian woman with black hair who kept asking him all about himself and about Breslauer and about his hopes for the future and his plans for seeing those hopes fulfilled.

He became enthralled by his own cover story. He became more detailed in his web-spinning. He wanted to marry, he told Lin, and have children. Children that he would never abandon the way he had been deserted. He wanted to adore his wife forever, and spare her all the pain his no-good father had bestowed on his mother. He was going to be a professor, he thought, just like the guy he was traveling with. One that new generations of students could admire and look up to.

Without at first realizing it, Roger was spinning out his tale as they walked along the beach. The pleasant buzz of the sugar liquor had obliterated his memory of exactly when they had paid the bill and stood up. Now he was with her, alone, the moon was shining brightly, the waves were crashing on the white, white sand.

She turned, stopping their walk, and looked at him. It seemed that in her eyes was as much pain as in the look of his fictitious mother when she bade him a tearful goodbye at the Reno airport. Lin's arms went around his shoulders and pulled him close to her. Her tongue, that same pink tongue that had made him crazy with desire back at the pool, darted out and moistened his lips, outlining them with its sweet taste.

He wrapped his arms around her waist and pulled her toward him. There was hunger, some primal need he felt, but it was held in check by the intuition that she was going to teach him something, something very important. He was supposed to stand still, and let her lead the way. He refused to act out the impulses that tugged desperately at all his muscles.

She moved her head away from him without actually having kissed him. He found that a delightful torment.

"You've had such a hard life for someone so young. So much pain . . ." She let her sentence linger, trail away from them; her hands moved gently back to his face. She framed his cheeks with her palms. He flinched when a wave of the rising tide crashed against their ankles, but she held him fast, in her strong grip.

She pressed toward him, and together they moved several feet inland, out of the range of the waves for at least a few minutes.

He was dizzy from the alcohol and the attention she was paying to him. Fantasy and reality, this exotic woman on a tropical beach, his cover story that had become so real, the sensation of her hands as they left his face and trailed down over his arms, his waist, to his hips, and then. . .

She was kneeling before him. Her hands were light, he could barely feel them at work as they easily undid his belt buckle and then softly slid down his zipper. She parted the slacks and he could feel them fall to the damp sand, leaving him there with only his shorts on, their white cotton soaking up the moonlight and clearly illuminating the curved bulge of his erection.

The shorts were the same size as the Speedos he'd worried about all day. Now, with the total flood of his excitement, his erection did what he had feared earlier—the enlarged bulb of its tip forced itself over the elastic band. Lin saw it, moved forward, and licked at the tight skin.

Roger moaned, his facade of control crumbling.

His hands went to her shoulders as though he needed them for support. But his grip was light, as though it was just the contact with her that was important. Now her hands tugged at the elastic waistband and pulled it down. He enjoyed a sudden sense of freedom as his erection was sprung free, waving in the warm tropical night air.

Then there was a burst of heat as her mouth moved over it. Unbelievably, she continued down the shaft. It felt enormous to Roger because it so much dominated his consciousness, but her mouth, that little mouth that held her tiny pink tongue, encased the whole of it. The sounds of her sliding and slipping back and forth were musical to him, perfectly accompanying the soft trade wind that whispered in the top-knots of the palm foliage.

He couldn't take it. The pleasure was so intense that he knew he would end it all if he allowed her to continue. He pulled back and then dropped to his own knees before her. He reached for her, brought her to himself and felt her breasts once more pressing against him. Their mouths were both open. They merged, the sweet taste of her saliva flowed into him.

He pushed her backward. She didn't resist. In a moment he was on top of her, his erection spearing into the cotton of her dress. One of his hands found the hemline and pulled it up, letting the hard shaft move against the silky flesh of her thighs and finding—as he'd so desperately hoped—the naked entrance.

Her legs moved skillfully to wrap around his waist. Her arms were pressing against his shoulder blades. There was no mistaking the invitation of her sucking mouth as it begged his tongue to enter her throat with wordless supplication. His erection moved toward her. He felt the soft hair around her mound, and then felt himself moving effortlessly between the wet and willing lips.

A groan escaped from between his clasped lips into her mouth as he continued to sink into her. He could feel her pubic hair now, tangling with his own. Her hands moved down and clamped onto his naked buttocks, urging him on.

He began slow thrusts, but her hands let him know there was no need for delicacy. This was a time for hunger, sheer hunger that had to be fed. It could only be satiated with one thing, the hard and immediate and hot pulsing of his hips. He plunged in and out with long and fast motions. His pelvis drove pistonlike as the length of his erection first entered, then withdrew, then returned, then retreated, again and again, so fast he knew he should slow down, so wonderfully he knew he couldn't stop.

Just when it was all becoming impossible, just when his first thoughts of insufficiency entered his mind, when he wondered if he could ever satisfy a woman like this, there was a firm and pulsing clamp on his erection, and he could feel her muscles spasming around him, trapping him inside her with warm waves of motion that were too much for him. His own orgasm crashed in on him, forcing him to arc his body up away from her, the tightness too much to control.

But Lin wouldn't let go. She lifted herself up, holding onto his shoulders, demanding that his chest keep contact against hers. Then it was over: all at once, it was done. They collapsed onto the sand, their mouths found each other and they began feeding again. The hunger was only teased, not close to satisfied. They couldn't possibly let one another go. Not now.

The moonlight gave him a chance to examine her body. He was entranced with it. There had only been one other time he'd had this kind of luxury of calm exploration . . . with Stasia. That memory swept over him fiercely. *The hurt won't go away.*

So live with it.

Before Lin had a chance to wonder about Roger's thoughts, he brought his hand down on one of her breasts. He cupped the warm, naked flesh. The small nipple was hard with excitement. As soon as his palm had made contact she let out a slight hiss of pleasure.

He leaned over and replaced his palm with his mouth, sucking in the dark-colored flesh, just as he had fantasized doing at the pool. He ran his tongue back and forth over the surface of it, pushing, then pulling the nipple's tip.

Lin's hands took hold behind his neck. A subtle motion hinted that he should move downward. His tongue led the way, leaving a slick line of liquid as his body followed her silent request. He lingered at her navel, letting his tongue dig deep into the small crevice there. Then, when her hands became more urgent, he went more quickly to the beginning of her pubic hair.

It was so unexpectedly soft. The short black hair wasn't kinky or curly the way occidental women's was. It lay flat on her belly in satiny waves. He flicked the pubic patch with his tongue, teasing her, slightly tickling. Then he let his mouth move farther down until it rested cautiously on the lips that guarded the pinkness inside her. That place that had so recently given him such incredible pleasure.

He thought she might want him to do more down there. He was ready to, wondering what it would taste like after their sex. Would it be different now that his own stuff was in there? But instead her hands pulled on him, lifting him back up to her.

She took his hand and then stood, her nude body open to his approving stare. She tugged again, motioning toward the water.

They stood, then ran toward the surf and ran in together. Off in the distance was the sound of the native drums still playing at the restaurant. Here, beside him, Lin Tao was nude, laughing and splashing him. He took her in his arms and once more had the thrill of her naked body pressed against his.

They stopped, frozen in their embrace. She looked up at him and they kissed. Suddenly the pounding ocean waves were silent. The music was gone. The moon had ceased to shine. There was only the heat and the noise of the blood moving in him once more, making him hard again, pressing his erection against her nether lips.

Even in the cooler Pacific water he could feel his erection expanding. It made him feel both powerful and vulnerable at the same time. That was *him*. The adult male reacting to the presence of this beautiful and compliant woman. A woman who was making her needs and desires perfectly clear right at the moment. Using the buoyancy of the water, she had wrapped her legs around his hips, her vagina opening to him, almost as though it would suck in his cock.

That was the vulnerability, the need that was apparent in his erection was some kind of weakness at the moment. But what a beautiful weakness, he thought.

He hefted Lin up further until she was straddling his waist. Her legs met behind him, the warm and fluid part of her burned against his belly. He carried her back onto the beach.

Now he spread her under the same tree as before. He knelt down between her splayed legs. His mouth nibbled quickly at her breasts. He only pecked her lips. He was interested in more than a sensual exploration this time.

His face buried itself between her thighs. The firm tone of those well-exercised muscles clamped his neck. His tongue was hungry. It moved hard and fast against the secret inner workings of her body. He was slightly disappointed that the only flavor there came from the ocean water. But that was hardly going to stop him now.

He wanted something that he thought he could get this way. He wanted . . . He wanted to know her need was as great as his. He wanted some equivalent to his erection to become apparent. There was some small groans from above him, cries that seemed to transform this Asian woman of the world, this lady who'd been his confessor, into a young girl. That was good. But not enough.

Then there were the hands gripping his hair again. They only drove his mouth on, making it move faster and making it push harder against her.

Then the moans turned to a stifled scream. Better. The hands began to pull at his hair. But only when they were pulling hard enough to cause him real pain did he believe her. Only then did he lift himself up. He was kneeling then, looking down at Lin, her mouth open, her pubic hair wet with his saliva.

"Please," she said.

That was what he wanted. He lifted her legs up with his hands, holding them far apart. He watched his erection as the plumlike head pushed apart her pubic lips. This was what he had been working for.

12

"DID YOU KEEP YOUR EYES open last night?" his father asked.

Roger had just opened those eyes to the blinding morning sun of Suparta. His father was standing by the bureau, pulling on his slacks, still shirtless.

It took Roger a moment to realize that his father was *not* referring to his encounter with Lin Tao on the moon-drenched beach.

"Yeah," he answered groggily, still not quite sure what his father *did* mean. "Yeah, sure I did." Roger yawned, tensed his muscles, and lifted himself up on his shoulder blades and heels, pressing against the cool sheet. He was suddenly aware of a morning erection under the covers. The idea that his father might see that was suddenly too embarrassing for Roger to contemplate.

"Time to get up," Michael Sheriff said. "I've already showered. Go ahead."

"In a minute, Dad, give me a minute." Roger rolled over and pulled the sheet up to his neck. How could he ever get rid of that hard-on while he could still smell Lin's perfume on his skin?

It had rubbed off on the pillow too. Christ, he hoped the chambermaid changed the linen, or he'd never get to sleep tonight.

"Roger!" Michael's voice was suddenly hard. "Come on! We have work to do."

"Dad, go on down to breakfast. I'll be right there."

"Roger, will you please . . ." Then, as though he suddenly understood what might be going on, Michael stopped talking. Roger didn't look up, but he could tell from the noise his father was making that Michael was moving faster to get dressed. "Sure, I'll get a table. Um, just make it quick, okay?"

"Sure."

Roger did hurry, and not just with his shower. He had to take care of the painful pressure of that erection before he could go down to the dining room. But he managed it all in record time. He appeared bright-eyed and enthusiastic, dressed in cotton slacks and a designer T-shirt.

"I ordered for you," Michael said, not looking up from the international edition of the *New York Times* he was reading.

"Thanks." Roger sat down and picked up a fork, playing with it on the tablecloth, uncertain how to handle all this with his father. Sex stuff was bad enough. But when your old man's in the next twin bed in your hotel room, it was sheer hell. No use asking for a separate room—they slept together not for companionship, and not to save money, but for mutual protection against possible enemy intrusion. But Roger couldn't feel badly about Lin. No way. That woman was too, too wonderful. Even though he'd just jerked off, Roger felt himself stirring in his pants.

A waiter appeared with a perfect American breakfast for each of them. Scrambled eggs, sausages, toast, orange juice, the works. The two Sheriff men went at their meals with gusto. Eating together was a lot easier than talking to one another at moments like this.

"You were already asleep when I got in," said Sheriff, glancing at his son over the rim of his cup.

"The change in time zones whacked me out," said Roger, who decided suddenly, at that moment, that he wasn't going to tell his father that he'd got laid. He didn't know why—he was just acting on instinct. "What time is it in Boston right now?"

"If you knew, you'd just get whacked out again. I got held up at the university. The grand tour. Dinner, speeches, the whole thing. I figured you could take care of yourself. I hope you put the time to use."

"Yes." Roger nodded. "I poked around a little. Got to know how the place smells."

That was MIS jargon, the kind that would probably impress the old man.

"Fine," said Sheriff, apparently satisfied. "When you're on your own like that, that's just what you're supposed to do. Tourist crap. Acting your cover. Getting into it. And keeping your eyes open. You never know what is going to come in handy on a mission like this."

They spoke in low voices so that they couldn't have been overheard by anyone sitting a couple of feet away.

"What did you find out?" Roger asked. "About the attacks?"

"They've lessened in the past week or so. Nothing for the last three days."

"That's good," said Roger.

"That's bad," said Sheriff. "It probably means one of two things: Somebody knows we're here and they're laying off for a while. Or it means that they're planning for something real big. In either case, it makes it just that much harder for us to find them. We need a trail, and the fresher it is, the easier it is to follow."

Roger nodded his understanding of this reasoning. "What's up today?"

"A tour of one of the factories on the north shore of the island. I met the owner at the banquet last night—apparently there's a big banquet at the university every week and everybody important on the island shows. We'll go by air. I hired a helicopter."

Roger loved the sound of that. He and his father had hired a chopper. He could imagine saying to Lin when he next saw her, *Professor Sheriff and I had a helicopter at our disposal* . . . "Sounds good," he said to his father. "What time?"

Michael looked at his watch. "Half an hour or so. We should get going."

After Michael signed the check with his name and room number, they went out into the sun and hailed one of the Peugeot cabs that were the most common vehicles in Pato Lako. They climbed in and the driver, who spoke in a singsong pidgin English, gladly drove off to the airport.

They had arrived at night, Roger had slept most of the next day, and the next evening he had spent in the company of Lin Tao—noticing not much except her for all that time. Now that he was seeing more of the island when he was fresh and awake, he was able to compare it to what he had studied on the videotapes. His father was right: It was exactly the same, and yet it was entirely different.

Suparta had to fight a constant battle against the rain forest that was desperate to regain its hold on the small amount of land that had been cleared for civilization. Flowers bloomed riotously in every ditch and out of every crack in building or road. These small plants were the forerunners of the vines, shrubs, and trees that would soon take over if given half a chance. The road to the airport was paved but uneven, with creeping plants that shot out from either side of the road, as if stretching to meet in the middle. As Roger looked out the taxi window he realized that the blazing sun overhead did not penetrate deeply into the forest. Down below the canopy of branches and vines, the earth was dark and dank, smelling of sweet rot, and loud with the cries of brightly plumed birds. It would have required a machete to penetrate the forest more than two or three feet from the road. This, he knew, was true of all the island landscape. Occasionally the forest was broken by cleared land, manioc or tuber farming, or even, in one place, a golf course. But a single season of neglect was sufficient for forest reclamation.

It was all beautiful, gloriously gaudy and beautiful.

The weather, the perfectly stable temperatures and the bright equatorial sun that made Suparta such a garden spot, the smell of seaweed and iodine every time the road came within view of the aquamarine Pacific waters, made the place seem an island Eden. It felt strange to wear clothes here. Especially not the long pants and underwear that he had on. Just a cotton shift perhaps, exactly what the natives wore—that would have been sufficient.

He wondered if his father ever thought about stuff like that. He turned to Michael and saw him watching out the other window—but his father was pressed back against the seat. No one watching from the road would have seen him in the shadows. An exotic forest with its exotic scents—and Michael Sheriff was guarding against snipers. Roger realized that his father saw this island Eden as nothing more than a battlefield, dense and green and surrounded by water, but a battlefield for all that. He had seldom seen his father enjoy things in a simple fashion. That perception struck him hard. It was difficult to realize and accept because it made him think in two conflicting manners: first, that the only time his father had been able truly to relax was the week they'd spent together in Maine; second, that it was precisely that hardness that had kept Michael Sheriff alive, and had put him in the position where he might inherit the Chairman's job and all the money and power that came with it.

Roger sank against the back of the seat. Maybe there *were* snipers. Was that what he needed to do to be an MIS operative—place himself in that line of inheritance? Become as steely cold as his father?

A surge of grief came over him. It was so strong and so painful he had to close his eyes for a moment. And when he did the image of Stasia was there, burning bright on the back of his eyelids. Oh God, that hurt. Could he have protected himself from that pain? It made him wince to think how unprotected, how unprepared he had been to

take on a mission of that importance. Compared to what
he knew now, then he had known nothing at all.

All the changes in thought. This place was affecting
him like he was on drugs.

The taxi slowed down. Roger opened his eyes and saw
they were pulling into the airport. The driver went beyond the gates where the international jumbo jets were
unloaded and continued on down the drive toward the old
terminal. *Island Flying Service* a large, hand-painted sign
read.

"Here you are, gentlesmen," the cab driver sang out.

13

MICHAEL PAID the driver. "This way," he said to Roger and walked toward the terminal. "I hired the 'copter for the day. We'll get where we're going—but we'll also get an overview of the island. Maps only go so far."

"What's the cover?"

Sheriff stared at his son. Wasn't anything getting through?

"Same one as this morning at breakfast. Same one as last night. Same one as on the plane coming over. Same one that we planned out in Boston. The cover is you're a student and I'm a professor. You're nice and quiet and I give the orders."

Roger swallowed a smirk of disgust, and said only, "Yes sir."

Michael wanted to hurl a fist into his son's face. But no, not now. Probably not ever. It wasn't just that Roger was being slow about this business—not thinking. It was that they were together every damn minute of the day. Too close. Much too close. This morning had been a perfect example. So damned embarrassing. The kid had a right to some privacy and a right to be taken seriously as well. Part of it was just the goddamn age thing. Here Roger was with a man's sex drive and an adolescent's insecurity; a boy's empty arrogance but an adult's solid job to perform. There was no way to keep all this in balance; no way at all. It just couldn't be done.

Roger was Michael's son. Roger was Michael's apprentice. Michael's responsibility. And Michael had to teach the son right, because it might be that the son would end up having to save his father's life.

That was too great a burden on the kid. That was all, this whole thing had gotten out of hand. Michael should never have let the Chairman and the kid gang up on him that way. Never. He should have insisted that Roger stay in school and that he not go on an assignment like this one. Not one so dangerous.

That was another problem, of course. All missions were dangerous. There would never be a right time.

They came to the grimy counter. It looked like a dozen men had stood there idly with knives whittling away at the edges of the discolored linoleum top. An American, mid-fifties, fat, was sitting behind an equally scarred desk several yards away.

"Help you?" he asked, without looking up.

"Dr. Sheriff," said Michael, speaking in a tone that was a pitch higher than his normal voice—softer, smoother, more professorial. "I called and reserved a helicopter for today."

"Oh yeah," said the man, laying his hand on some stapled documents. He only looked at them as he stood up. His rotund belly bulged over his waistline; his belt was swung in an arc below it. He wore a Hawaiian print shirt, with the slick material pulling apart across his chest, straining at the buttons. "Hey Sheila!" he called. "Here's your fare!"

From behind a curtain a little distance off a woman yelled back, "Coming."

The American man reached the counter's edge, and dropped the forms on the surface. He glanced at them again to make sure he got the name right. "Sheriff, wasn't it?" He glanced at Roger.

Roger returned the gaze steadfastly—as if squaring off against a possible adversary.

Oh Christ, thought Michael. He nudged his son's foot with the side of his shoe. *Don't give it away, jerk.*

Michael pulled out a credit card, and pushed it across the desk. The man, glancing curiously at Roger, made out the slip and passed it back across. He didn't bother calling it in, or verifying the card against a list. "You'll be in the air in no time. *Sheila!*"

This time a body pushed through the curtains.

A good body.

In the States she would have been more than passable with brown hair and a long figure and smooth skin. But here in the tropics her hair had been lightened and streaked by the sun. Her long figure was stretched and supple and there wasn't much covering it—just cut-off jeans and a printed halter top of thin cotton. Her smooth skin was dark, and didn't show any change of color at the edges of her clothing. Always a good sign, that.

"Sheila Doles," she announced, throwing out a hand to Michael. "You ready?" She only glanced at Roger, treating him as an assistant who wasn't going to have a say. Roger didn't like it, but it showed that the cover worked.

That was Michael's first impression at least. But as he saw Sheila's lingering eyes sweep his own chest he realized he might have begun a new little conquest for himself. Little? A major conquest. Sheila moved slightly, letting her breasts shift in the halter top, the small nubs of her nipples showing through the cloth. Whatever the chemistry that works between men and women, it was going for the two of them right now.

"Best pilot on the islands," said the big-bellied man, waddling back to his desk. His praise was unenthusiastic, but seemed sincere. Of course, how many pilots—male or female—could there be on an island this size?

"Let's go," she said. "Anybody afraid of heights?"

Roger snorted in derision, but Michael stopped him with a quick glare. "I'll be fine," said Sheriff. "This is my assistant, Roger Baynter."

The woman pilot gave a quick nod to Roger. "So long, Dad. Keep the pots hot. I'll be back sometime."

Father and daughter operation.

They followed Sheila Doles out the door of the shack onto a tiny runway that wasn't more than beaten grass.

"Oh, shit," Roger breathed. "A woman pilot. 'Copter's older than I am."

It probably was. A Bell 500, it was probably Army surplus left over from the Vietnam War. *Island Flying Service* had been painted red on the door with a spray canister.

"Don't worry about it," said Sheriff. "If that's her father, she was born and raised here and has been flying since she was ten. If that's the helicopter she learned to fly in, she'll fly it like I drive my Volvo."

Sheila had gone around and hoisted herself instantly into the pilot's seat. She pushed open the other door for Professor Sheriff and his sullen assistant. Michael took the seat beside her.

"This is a whole-day affair, right?" she asked as she engaged the engine.

"Yes."

"Then you obviously want more than a quick ride to the north shore. What's your pleasure?" The big rotary blades swung slowly into life.

"Show me everything," said Sheriff. "I'm interested in the overall picture. Not looking for anything in particular. But I take it you know the island—"

She laughed, not even bothering to answer.

"—and I'd appreciate getting the guided tour."

Roger was being ignored in the back, leaning forward between the pilot and his father. Michael just hoped that he realized this was part of the cover. For this trip he was to play the part of Roger Fetch-and-Carry, and beyond that he was to keep his mouth shut, like the paid student assistant he was supposed to be.

"Here's the list," said Roger, handing it forward.

Sheriff tried to grab it, but Sheila Doles had already snagged it. A map of the island was marked with a dozen locations, and lines had been drawn connecting the points in an orderly fashion.

Sheila ran a finger along the itinerary. "You want the highest mountains. You want the deepest valleys. And you want the location of every single major military and industrial plant on the goddamn island. I guess that is the overall picture."

"We're studying religion," piped Roger.

"Right," said Sheila, glancing at Sheriff.

Michael thought Sheila's evaluation was more than passingly sharp. Because of Roger's eagerness to be in this scene, he'd have to play his part even more carefully. "Yes, I am studying religion," he said, "but from a very specific point of view. The influence of geography on the development and sustenance of primitive, and especially of sun-worshipping, cults. Suparta is an ideal setting for my research. Small island, long-established religion, even some written records. But an intimate knowledge of the landscape is a crucial factor in my ability to carry out my program of intended research."

Sheila looked at him dubiously. "Right," she said again. "Factories and military units play a major part of ancient sun-worship, I guess."

Sheriff replied, "I heard that there were regular helicopter flights from Pato Lako to the factories and the military installations. I wanted to see if it wouldn't be possible for me to take advantage of that." Then, to change the subject quickly, he remarked, "I've heard there are some quite spectacular ruins."

"You haven't marked them on the map," she said, glancing at the page again, and studying the printing at the edges of the photoduplicated page to see what the origin of it was. She turned the map right side up. "The ruins are here, here, and here. Or thereabouts. We'll fly over—but only if you're interested, of course."

"That's why we're here," Roger said blithely.

"Most of the ruins are . . . well, in ruins. Nobody believes that hype anymore. Even the Supartan priests hang out in Satuka at the university. The university has indoor plumbing. Ruins in the middle of the rain forest don't have indoor plumbing. They don't even have roofs.''

With that, she revved up the engines. The airport was apparently without traffic, but still Sheila went through the routine of calling the tower to get clearance. The ''tower'' was not much more than ten feet off the ground, and it was about to be pulled down a whole lot lower by a climbing vine that was covered in yellow flowers.

''You got it, Sheila,'' came the voice over the radio. ''Who you got today?''

Sheila looked at Sheriff, who said nothing, and betrayed nothing with his face. But out of the corner of his eye, he could see alarm in his son's eyes.

''Nobody,'' said Sheila, and flicked the radio off. ''Joy ride.''

. . . *14*

WITH GREAT EASE the Bell 500 lifted up off the square of concrete next to the runway. Soon the airport was lost to sight, as were all other traces of civilization. As they flew along over the dense, unbroken forest, Sheila gave a running commentary.

"Suparta's pretty big for this part of the world. Most of the islands are just tips of volcanos that rise up off the ocean floor. But this is a real land mass. They tell me it must have broken off from New Guinea a few tens of millions of years ago. I don't know about that sort of thing. Always makes me feel strange to hear people talk about land tearing off the edge of continents and moving around, like it was a child going off on its own."

Michael Sheriff couldn't resist glancing at his son at this remark. Roger had on his attentive-student face, and didn't notice. Or at least didn't react.

"But it's here," Sheila went on. "All of it in all its glory. How the place stayed out of World War II, I'll never know. I guess it was a combination of things. First, everybody was a little afraid of it—the natives are independent, they always have been, and they'd made it clear that they'd fight interference to the last man. As you can see, there's plenty of room for guerilla operations. This makes the Vietnam jungle look like a plowed field."

"You were in Vietnam?" Roger asked. Michael was glad: It was the question he himself wanted to ask.

"Cavalry Medvac."

Michael was impressed, and even more interested. No wonder this lady was sharp. They exchanged glances: hard glances of appraisal. He wondered if she believed for a minute that he was a professor of religion from Breslauer University. Probably not. But she was smart, and she was acting as if that was what he was. But her eyes and her wicked smiles told another story. She was waiting to see what she could find out.

"The second reason," Michael prompted.

"What?"

"The second reason that Suparta didn't get into World War II?"

Sheila grinned. "There wasn't anything here anybody wanted. And it's still pretty secure. Got a few old buildings from the time when there were these great kings—"

"There still is a king," Roger interrupted. "I've got his name right here somewhere. He—"

"Figurehead," said Sheriff quickly. Now Roger was showing off his research. Goddamn, why didn't the kid just *shut up?*

Sheila seemed to take no note of the interruption. "The people are good. Easygoing for the most part, but for some goddamn reason they also make good workers. The perfect combination. I've taken tours of the factories. The people who work there are happy as clams, because they get air conditioning, and they show free American movies, and they all seem to look on the work as some sort of game. You know, the 'Can You Get All The Wires Attached Properly So The Light Lights Up' sort of game."

Sheriff laughed. "Sounds like a wicked industrialist's dream of a society: cheap, docile, energetic labor. This island have any problems?"

"You're looking at it."

Nothing but forest below them.

"Jungle?" asked Roger.

"The forest is the enemy. The thing's alive, and you turn your back—it takes over. Slash-and-burn doesn't work here. The forest comes right back in. It's a little better now with mechanical farm machinery, and there is *some* farming—but still there are no major interior settlements. When I show you the ruins, you'll see that they were all built on bare outcroppings of rock—the only place on the island, besides the beaches, where the jungle hasn't quite managed to take over.''

Underneath the helicopter the trees were a solid mass of green. Here and there large black birds sailed in brief silhouette against the blue sky. When the Sheriffs had been driving along the highway toward the airport, the jungle had been dotted with flowers, and the black rotting space below the green tops was crisscrossed with yellow vines. But from up here, they saw only rolling lush greenery.

Then, quickly, the hills started to rise. Michael could sense them first when he noticed the treetops undulating upward.

Then there were cliffs. Sheer hundred-foot heights of reddish crumbling rock. On the plateau above the cliffs, the forest began again, thick and green as below. A block of earth had suddenly been shifted upward, drastically and probably by earthquake, Sheriff assumed.

''And here's why Suparta's important now,'' Sheila resumed. ''This plateau. Thousands of square miles of absolutely level ground, covered with unbroken, impenetrable forest. You're on the Equator practically, you've got clear skies, you've got safety from intrusion, you've got secrecy.''

''Secrecy?'' echoed Roger.

Sheila nodded. ''There are satellite tracking stations all right. But I also suspect there's other stuff out here, too.''

''What sort of stuff?'' Roger pursued.

Sheila glanced at Sheriff, and then shrugged: ''How would I know?''

She banked the chopper left. ''Here we go. The tracking stations. I get a kick out of it. They're all in a row. There, there's the first one." Sheila pointed nearly straight ahead.

At first all Michael could see was a break in the trees, then after a moment he caught the first glimpse of bare ground he'd seen since they'd left the airport. A large diamond-formation of satellite dishes was spread out over the clearing, and in the corner was a long, low concrete structure, painted dark blue. An American flag waved above it.

As quickly as he'd taken that in, Sheila veered off again.

"Close enough," Sheila said. Unspoken, but in her tone was, *They shoot.* "Twenty miles on, you got Japan. Ten after that is New Zealand. Then ten more is the European Space Agency. Wild, I tell you, wild. They don't trust each other even that much—and all these guys are supposed to be allies. You'd think they'd get together, even if it was just to play cards, but they don't."

"How do you know that?" Sheriff asked casually.

"If they even talked to each other on the radio," said Sheila, "we'd sometimes pick it up. But they don't. They only talk to home, and they scramble."

"So you think there's more to these installations than just satellite tracking?" Sheriff asked.

"I think there's probably some sort of research going on out here, that's all. I don't think that Suparta is a major nuclear arsenal or anything like that. Just research of some sort—there's not room for anything else. Anyway, the government at Satuka doesn't care. They get half a dozen rents instead of one. And those rents are high, let me tell you."

In the next half-hour, she took them by the other four installations, and Sheriff and Roger gazed at them out of the windows of the helicopter.

"Now," said Sheila, banking the plane to the north. "I'll show you the stuff you're *really* interested in."

They flew for another thirty miles, over jungle so compact that it made the isolated tracking stations seem areas of dense population in comparison. But they remained on the plateau. The sea was a distant hazy blue line.

Sheila was alternately looking carefully out the window and glancing at her instruments, as if the place she was looking for were difficult to find—more difficult than the tracking stations, certainly, for she'd gone right for them, without checking anything.

Then she grinned and pointed, but that was unnecessary because Michael Sheriff had already seen it. Another clearing on the plateau. But this one didn't have the green floor of lawn or the fields with arrays of dishes the others possessed. And Sheila was able to fly directly over it.

An irregular square of land, covered with what looked to be pitted concrete. And instead of radar dishes and low painted buildings there were only stone ruins—the remains of an oval temple. It was faintly green, probably a result of some covering of fungus.

"Is that concrete?" Sheriff asked, puzzled.

"The forest tears up concrete like it was peanut brittle," said Sheila. "That's *salt,* the only thing that keeps the forest back. That's one of the mysteries of this place—how the hell the salt got up here. That salt must have been laid down ten feet thick, to keep the forest back this long. Probably the priests had the whole population of the island down at the ocean evaporating sea water for a hundred years to get this much salt—and then they had to get it up here."

"People do weird things for religion," Roger commented sententiously from the back.

Michael was a little unnerved, and requested that Sheila fly over the place again. This temple hadn't been in any of the reports prepared by MIS.

Sheila hovered low, and Michael and Roger peered out.

"Have you ever been down there?" Roger asked.

"Don't want to chance it," said Sheila. "I *might* make

it, but it still looks to me like the blades would either swipe the temple or the tree line. Either way, I'd be stuck. And no taxi service from here back to Pato Lako. I imagine the place is impossible to get to on the ground as well. Probably nobody's been down there for a hundred years.''

Roger started to speak, but Michael Sheriff turned sharply and silenced his son with a look. Michael knew what Roger was going to say, and he didn't want him to say it. Roger was about to say, *But there's somebody down there now.*

Michael knew, too, that Roger was right, for Michael had seen the furtive shadow of the man on one of the long curved walls of the ruined temple.

LIN TAO HAD ALREADY taken her helicopter ride. She stood now on the landing pad watching her craft lift up and move back toward Pato Lako. As soon as the rotary blades had cleared the tops of the trees there was another mechanical noise. Within a minute a camouflaged tarpaulin had been locked into place, and no one flying over would be able to discern the clearing.

Lin Tao moved to the edge of the clearing. There was a house there. The density of the surrounding vegetation masked the extent and size of this unadorned structure.

A somber servant opened the door for Lin Tao and moved aside to allow her easy entrance. She nodded, not with civility, but simply to acknowledge the action.

Then Lin Tao moved to a room just beyond the entrance hall. It was a plain-looking space, white walled, with modern Western furniture and a few suggestions that the occupants might be Chinese. A centuries-old blue and white vase stood on a corner table; on the walls were scrolls painted before the West even knew there was a China; in one corner was a carved and gilded statue of a storm deity, four feet high.

At a table in another corner of the room sat a middle-aged man with an abacus before him. The counters moved with rhythmic clicking.

"Did you find yourself some diversion?" he asked. The abacus counters still clicked. He had not looked up.

"Yes." Lin Tao sat down on a modern leather and

chrome chair. A silent servant appeared with tea in a pot, and two cups beside it on the tray. He placed it on the low table in front of her. She poured for herself, and said nothing to the servant, who went away silently.

"Young?" The voice inquired again, this time with a hint of teasing in it.

"Very young, father." Lin Tao sipped at the hot drink.

The man put the abacus aside and stood. He was wearing a three-piece Western-style suit. The room was air conditioned and without windows. It was impossible to know how close the jungle was. He seated himself across from Lin Tao and poured the second cup of tea.

"What news?" he asked.

"I went to a luncheon at the British Embassy yesterday. The chargé d'affaires told me that the Nanking Banking Corporation is moving its charter from Hong Kong to the Bahamas. Word will be leaked soon. Maybe as soon as tomorrow. It will cause great upheaval, no doubt."

The man stiffened. "Why is it that the inevitable still causes me to be so surprised?" he asked, but in a tone of voice that didn't solicit a reply. He shook his head. "The British are fools, giving up Hong Kong to the Communists. The disruption it will cause!"

"To the international banking world? Are you really so worried about that, Father?"

Lao Chiang smiled. "Actually, we have fairly significant investments in Hong Kong banks."

"But not nearly as significant as we have here."

"Our investments here are minor, from a monetary point of view at least. It's the potential that's staggering."

"Have you gotten back the results of the soil samples?"

"Yes, yes." He smiled much more broadly now. "There'll be no problem with that. The soil, the climate, all of it is perfect."

"More perfect than Hong Kong?" Lin Tao asked.

Her father shook his head sadly. "It is the city of our ancestors. Our traditions are there. But here in Suparta we have an opportunity that Hong Kong never presented to us. For the first time in decades, we can control the sources of our supplies."

"If we can control the natives," Lin Tao added.

"We Chinese have always had such respect for the old traditions." The man smiled again. "We are not like the Occidentals who come in and try to supplant them. We, of all people, have learned to take the modern and make it enrich the ancient, daughter. By 1999, when the British are foolish enough to leave Hong Kong in the hands of the Communists, then we will have done our jobs as the guardians of an ancient people in need of the resurrection of their heritage."

Lin Tao laughed. "Sometimes, Father, I almost believe you when you talk that way. I could imagine that you think you are becoming your facade, that you are believing the foolishness you tell these people."

Lao Chiang didn't join her laughter. "You would do well to approach the same place, Lin Tao. You have become Goddess of the Moon to these people. It is no small part to play, and you must act it out faultlessly. Fanatical religious believers are an intolerant audience if you disappoint their expectations. They must never, *ever* suspect that you have laughed at their traditions and superstitions. Do you understand, Lin Tao?"

"Yes, Father," the young woman replied submissively.

. . . 16

AFTER HAVING FLOWN over and past all the designated interior areas on Michael Sheriff's small map, Sheila Doles turned the 'copter northward, and they flew toward the coast. Roger watched out the window eagerly for signs of civilization, but none appeared until the very last. A few villages on the very margin of the sea. Small villages with compounds of low factorylike buildings nearly connecting them.

"They don't just look like factories," Sheila told them, "they are factories. Electronics. Japanese, French, American, you name it. Once they discovered that Supartans work hard and aren't easily distracted, they landed here like locusts. The island got lots and lots of jobs out of it. Lots of immigrants too, people looking for high wages that they can't get in their own countries. You've got Singapore drawing people north, and Suparta drawing them south."

In just a few moments they were on land, a helicopter landing site—big enough to accommodate half a dozen birds—carved out of the jungle. The professional taxi drivers of Pato Lako weren't in evidence here, however. Just a single vehicle was waiting at the side of the airstrip. Sheila waved to the driver, and he rolled the cream-colored sedan over.

The driver was Japanese. He climbed out of the car, bowed slightly, and asked, "For Mr. Susaki?"

Sheriff nodded, then turned to Sheila: "Care to join

me? Mr. Susaki asked me to bring along whomever I pleased."

Sheriff and Sheila got into the back seat; Roger—still playing the peon student assistant whose opinion was not sought on anything—sat in the front with the driver.

"That's the ICDM facility," said Sheila, pointing at a high white windowless concrete structure as they passed it. "Some sort of ore processing, I'm not sure what. My metallurgy's about as strong as my grasp of religion, and I didn't even think that Suparta had ores. Just sand and about a million feet of rotted vegetation. Anyway, it's the Japanese electronics that are wild."

Michael looked at her. Wild? What did that mean? The driver sped along the road and talked in the strange local pidgin. Michael could have made it out with difficulty, but Sheila was an easy translator. They wove through a carefully planned set of small villages—the ones they'd seen from the air. This Michael did know about. The Supartan government had welcomed the foreign investors with open arms, but it had also stipulated that they not concentrate their plants in the two cities of the island. The Supartan regime didn't want Satuka and Pato Lako overwhelmed by development at the expense of the rest of the country, nor did it want tourists to see complexes of state-of-the-art electronics factories every time they looked out of their hotel windows in this island paradise.

The island government also didn't want shanty towns or instant slums. So they had insisted that each company establishing here also build a village for the housing of the workers. Each small township was to be separated from the others by some distance, to preserve that sense of community that Supartans were used to.

Half this northern shore of the island—out of the way of the monsoon track—had been built up in this fashion. A single two-lane road and a fleet of lorry buses connected the townships and factories. At the western extremity of this development, on a splendid spit of land jutting out into the sea, was a development of luxury homes for the foreign executives of the different factories.

It was all just one more example of the careful planning of the Supartan government. Sheriff looked on appreciatively. This was how a nation should maintain itself. Thoughtfully, forthrightly, with controlled development.

But there were some problems that all the planning in the world couldn't forestall.

The Susaki Mega-Byte factory came as a shock after the twenty-minute drive from the small airstrip. It was a building of two stories, the length and width of a football field. Designed in a shockingly modern style, it had stark white outer walls decorated with sudden blotches of bright pastels, all shining blindingly in the Supartan sun.

Michael Sheriff took in the dimensions of the building and the care with which the grounds around it had been maintained. In the Supartan climate the carefully trimmed lawn, unmarred by weeds, was something of a miracle, the kind of environmental miracle that the Japanese were known for.

An American firm would have been satisfied with the short-cut lawn. But Mega-Byte had installed a beautiful rock garden along one side of the factory. With small, trimmed shrubs, rock paths, and a system of artificial pools and running water, there was no question that this was a Japanese factory.

They walked to the front door. Just inside, a woman receptionist rose to greet them in traditional fashion, bowing silently before asking their business.

"We're here to see Mr. Susaki," Michael Sheriff said. He gave the receptionist his name and listened while the Japanese woman spoke softly into the telephone.

"He will be right with you. If you will have a seat."

Michael watched as both Roger and Sheila took in the atmosphere of the place. He hoped that studious expression on his son's face was reflective of an agent-in-training studying an interior as a possible arena for action, and not just Roger thinking of getting laid.

The reception room was large, paneled in some dark tropical wood that Michael couldn't identify. On the wall were long, narrow hand-painted scrolls depicting mountain tigers and bandits. The air was cool, air conditioned obviously, but he didn't detect either drafts or vents.

Mr. Susaki appeared quickly. When he came through the door, Sheriff noted trouble on the man's face, but it was wiped away instantly. If he hadn't happened to be looking in exactly the right direction, Michael wouldn't have seen that fleeting expression at all. But Mr. Susaki was the quintessential Japanese businessman and whatever was bothering him could not be allowed to interfere with his offer of hospitality. "Mr. Sheriff, it is a pleasure." Susaki went on with his obviously practiced speech.

Michael Sheriff replied in kind, then went on to introduce Roger and Sheila. But as he did so, he was thinking about Susaki's manner. There was something definitely wrong, something that couldn't be covered up with the habits of a lifetime of politeness.

Sheriff had admired the man at the university dinner the night before. He had been smart and quick and articulate. Too many Japanese, in their desire to emulate American modern success, had taken on some of the worst elements of American chauvinism as well. They acted like the colonial masters in countries like Suparta, disdaining the native culture and insisting that the locals adapt to an imposed Japanese style.

Susaki had been outspoken in his defense of the Supartan way of life. There must be ways, he had told Sheriff, for the Supartans to continue to benefit from the best in modern technology without having to integrate the worst offenses of American and Japanese consumerism.

The government, which Sheriff knew all about, but let Susaki explain nonetheless, had been doing a fine job. The Prime Minister, Makana Lako, was especially astute concerning such issues as the location of housing. It was his own policies which had established the system of small villages on this shore of the island and it was he who had refused to allow foreign investors to take the more efficient, and far cheaper, alternatives of high-rise buildings.

But, as did all leaders dealing with such issues, Makana Lako had problems separating the symbols of decadence from the reality. There was the pressure from the university students to allow modern music on the state radio. There were people who thought that there was even easier money to be made with big Western-style gambling casinos. Besides all of that, there had been a constant pressure from the various world powers to either open up Suparta even more—or else to turn it over to one particular power, for ''safe-keeping.''

But that had been an eloquent Susaki last night. The man who led them through the doors into the main area of the building was tentative, distracted, concerned with something far weightier than a guided tour for the pleasure of a visiting American scholar. Sheriff had the distinct impression that Susaki would have been delighted to avoid this appointment altogether, if he could have done so with politeness.

They walked down a plain, spotless corridor. The lights were bright overhead, but Sheriff could detect no dust in the air. When they reached a door at the end, Susaki said, ''I am afraid that I will have to ask you to cover your hair and clothes. We provide masks and overalls for visitors. The smallest particles of dust could render useless the delicate instruments we manufacture here.''

They entered a kind of windowless vestibule. The door sang mechanically shut behind them. The three visitors removed their shoes, and Susaki distributed disposable paper outfits. When they'd zipped up, Susaki apologetically made an inspection of each. Then came a covering for their hair, something like a shower cap. Finally a gauze mask for their mouths and noses.

Only when they had all passed muster—Susaki included—did the Japanese industrialist open the final door. There, in carefully calibrated lines, were table upon table of native workers, mostly women. They were hunched over their delicate tasks, and Sheriff heard no talking. Soft Western music played in the background.

They were like any other high-tech workers in the world except for one startling difference. The only coverings on any part of their bodies were the same mask and caps that the three Americans wore. When he looked closely Michael could see that the women also wore narrow flesh-colored G-strings about their mid-sections—but that was definitely all. Other than that, they were nude.

"The Supartans are, of course, not afflicted with Western modesty," Susaki explained matter-of-factly. "They prefer working this way, and in terms of the degree of sanitation required by our manufacturing procedures, bare skin is as acceptable as these paper suits. They scrub before entering, much as a doctor does before surgery, and that is sufficient for their seven-hour shifts."

Row upon row of naked breasts appeared as they strolled down the aisle, with each rank turning and bowing slightly to their employer as he passed with the Western visitors. It was strangely unerotic to Michael. No, not strangely. Most things in his business were, actually. When he was in this mode he was only partially aware of the attractiveness of women like these. He was much more likely to pay attention to a woman like Sheila Doles—as much for her skill as a pilot and her knowledge of the island as for her physical splendor. Sheila was the sort of woman who often came in very handy on missions. All these naked women registered, yes, but it was put into a memory store for later—a more appropriate time. Roger would have to learn that.

"Your tongue is dragging on the floor," Sheila said

quietly to Roger, and Michael was hard put to suppress a smile as he listened to Susaki.

After the industrialist had given details on the working conditions of these women, their unique educational backgrounds, and their remarkable skill at detail, the three visitors were led back out of the manufacturing unit. The door closed behind them again, and the paper suits were discarded.

Roger's eyes were still wide and astonished at what he'd seen inside.

Susaki led them into a kind of executive suite then, and a secretary served tea and some sort of flat, tasteless cake. Susaki kept up his lecture, but Sheriff could tell that the man's mind was elsewhere.

The industrialist looked relieved when a man—another Japanese—entered, whispered a couple of words to him, and then stood silently aside, waiting.

"Mr. Sheriff," said Susaki suddenly, "perhaps if the lady and young gentleman would excuse us, I could show you something along your own lines of specialty."

Michael Sheriff caught the alarm in Roger's eyes. Roger evidently thought that when Susaki said "your specialty," it meant he had torn away their cover. Michael shut up his son with a quick look that was lost on Susaki, but not on Sheila. "Certainly," Michael said, and rose.

The Japanese man who'd entered smiled a cold polite smile and held out his arm. Sheila and Roger preceded him out the door.

When they were alone, Susaki hesitated. He poured out more tea for himself and Sheriff. Sheriff ignored the cup before him: *Let's get down to business.*

"It was not my intention to intrude on your pleasant visit to our operation, but there is a matter which has come up, one on which I would like to ask your opinion as an expert."

"My expertise is primitive religion," said Sheriff.

"Just so."

It was evident to Sheriff that Susaki was not talking about whatever it was that had occupied his mind this noontime. But it hardly seemed likely that a major Japanese executive was going to be preoccupied by some question of theology.

Or was it?

"This island, Suparta, as you know, has progressed far. We had our conversation last evening . . ."

Sheriff waved away any further description of that. The damn Japanese politeness could force this conversation to go on for an hour. Something was going on. Sheriff wanted to know what it was.

"But Suparta is evidently not immune to many of the same currents of social change that are afflicting much greater, much more industrialized nations. You, in your country, have them, and so do we in Japan. The ultra-conservatives, the ones who would try and impose a medieval concept of war as a way of life on a modern industrialized society."

This was interesting. Sheriff leaned forward. "How is this affecting you? Here in Suparta?"

"The old ways—the ways of the people who were here for centuries, before there was any international trade in Suparta—are strange. They resemble an especially primitive medieval concept. You must—of all people on this island right now—be aware of the speculations that there is a connection between the ancient race of Suparta and the Aztecs and Incas?"

"Of course."

"The national religion was supposed to have been taken over from them. Now that's thought"—he paused for the right English word—"quaint. But the traditions linger. It is not unlike some parts of the Caribbean, or Australia, where utterly educated persons still cling to the ideas of voodoo, or still believe in the power of a shaman to direct life and to cause death."

Sheriff nodded.

"That," said Susaki, "and the Supartans have a rich

mythological tradition. Colorful tales that now are taught as native literature in the university. Yet whenever there is some sign to indicate that there might be truth to those tales, the more superstitious of the islanders become convinced, overnight, that the entire island ought to turn back to the old religion as the way of truth and life.''

Susaki paused, and looked out the window. ''The Supartans believe that there are demons living in the deepest parts of the forest. They are the demons who were here 'before the gods' and, by implication, they *are* gods. Demigods in the mythology, actually. Servants of the sun, who live in the tops of the jungle trees.''

Susaki had risen and gone over to a closet. He opened it and drew out a small box which he brought over to the table. He set it down, and Sheriff peered inside.

There was a pile of human figures crudely fashioned of stick and yarn.

''Those are Eye-of-the-Sun fetishes,'' said Michael. ''Totems of a demon people. But they're Aztec.''

''They're also Supartan,'' returned Susaki. ''The islanders believe they are omens of an invasion of the demon demigods. A warning of the time when the angry demons will leave the forests and attack humankind.''

Sheriff picked one of the dolls up, and turned it in his hand. Crude, hand-fashioned.

''They were found on the lawn this morning by security,'' said Susaki quietly. ''If any of my highly skilled, highly educated workers had seen these dolls, Mr. Sheriff, they would have abandoned my employ immediately. And never come back.''

Sheriff nodded. ''Anything else?''

''Not here,'' said Susaki. ''But at IMDC. You have heard of them?''

''Yes,'' Sheriff replied noncommittally. He certainly wasn't going to say that International Multi-Development Corporation was paying for this jaunt of his.

''There was an accident at the plant last week. A freak accident. A wall gave way, though subsequently no fault was found with the construction. Seven men were killed. My workers were upset, because the accident had been foretold in the village."

"Foretold?"

"The old ones—parents and grandparents of my young workers—were telling stories again, stories my workers had not heard since they were children. There is opposition to this industrial development. The demon-gods in the treetops are angry."

"This has happened before," said Sheriff. "In other places."

"I know," Susaki agreed sadly. "In Burma and Kampechka every trained professional the army could find was murdered. Scientific progress was antipolitical. The ability to read was a death warrant under Pol Pot. Of course," he added hastily, "I do not for one moment believe that things will *ever* be that bad in Suparta."

Right. That's what the United States said about Khomeni's revolution in Iran. Before that progressive nation was hurled back centuries under the iron-fisted leadership of a religiously reactionary regime.

17

THERE WAS A MESSAGE—marked *Extremely Urgent*—waiting for Michael Sheriff when he and Roger returned to the Royal Supartan. It demanded that he telephone the embassy immediately. He sent Roger up to the room and called from the lobby. Evidently the underlings had been expecting the call because he got through to the ambassador without any difficulty.

"Sheriff, did you get any real background for that idiotic cover of yours?" Maxwell Barton wasn't one for polite preliminaries.

"You know about how well MIS prepares for the field," he said quietly.

"Right," he said, "you've always got the right equipment. Like that little friend you brought along for companionship."

"What do you want, Maxwell?"

"I want your ass over here pronto."

Sheriff was silent for a moment.

"Please."

"Anything for a friend," said Michael, and hung up.

The men were arranged in a semicircle of straight chairs in front of the ambassador's massive desk. Barton waved Michael into the only empty place, at the end of the arc. The fact that he didn't introduce Sheriff meant, first, the ambassador was still trying his best to insult him; and second, that all the other men had at least an inkling of who Michael was and whom he represented.

Barton didn't say a word. He opened up a desk drawer and held something up: a yarn and stick figure—an Eye of the Sun.

"What is it?" he asked the company at large.

The men looked at one another. No one answered.

"Sheriff?"

"Where did you find it?" Michael asked.

"There were a dozen of them around the U.S. tracking installation this morning," replied one of the men nervously. He wore an Army uniform—a major—and it seemed probable he was stationed there. "The native workers saw them, turned right back around and went inside their compound, and wouldn't come out again. My men didn't get breakfast this morning."

Other of the representatives in the group were obviously CIA, and Sheriff knew that not only because of the connection of Barton with that organization. These men *stank* CIA. The operatives were uneasy. They had nothing to say, and they shuffled their feet on the carpet. Probably suffering with memories of another country, and another embassy: Teheran.

"Is it nothing?" demanded Barton. "Or is it a lot? That's all I want to know."

"It's *nothing*." One of the CIA men stood up suddenly. "I told you, Mr. Ambassador, there is no situation in Suparta that the military or civilian intelligence networks can't handle. Any five of my men could take over the whole damn island in two hours if it came down to that."

"Sheriff?" he asked, turning to him slowly.

"The CIA can't handle their own dicks to shake off after a piss," Michael remarked quietly.

The CIA men burned crimson, and the leader, already standing, made an angry motion toward Sheriff.

"Sit down," Barton ordered. "This isn't a sandbox for you boys to fuck around in. On this island is a top-level American scientific installation. I'm responsible for it. I will be the one to make the decision to send home the civilians, and it will be my decision to blow that god-damn place sky-high before anybody else gets his hands on that equipment, and when we find out who laid these things out there, it will be me who tells you, 'Go after those fuck-holes.' "

"You can't destroy that station. Not because of some childish totems." The man who spoke now wasn't one of the members of the security forces, Michael knew. He had a soft belly, thinning hair, and a wheeze in his voice—asthma.

"This is Dr. Pritchaird, head of the scientific team at the installation," Barton explained grudgingly. "Dr. Pritchaird, I'm not about to close down that station on this kind of threat." He tossed the totem aside with contempt. "But I wanted to know just how serious this could be. Nobody on this shit-hole island is going to come sneaking up on *my* ass, and *nobody* is going to get their grubby little hands on the kind of equipment you have out there while it's under *my* protection."

It's a spy station.

He'd suspected it, of course. From the beginning. But now that surmise was confirmed. He was only surprised that MIS hadn't known about it. He thought that through. There must be enough civilian data being sent out of there to make a perfect cover. Then, on the side, the rest of the material was being transmitted, probably triple-scrambled and through a long array of intermediaries, back to Washington. The station probably serviced two entirely separate species of satellites; the ones for international communication on one hand, and then the ones for the most secret of the Asian spy stations on the other. A very interesting target for someone. Hell, for anybody.

"All right, Sheriff, I didn't bring you in here to twiddle your dick. I want to know what you know. And I want to know it now."

He paused only a moment, then told them. He gave information about the totems' recent appearances in the industrial complexes and villages on the north shore of the island. He could have kept silent, but there was nothing in that information that would be of help to the others. He counted—correctly—on their lack of imagination.

Michael then gave out the history of the Supartan religion, greatly simplified, of course, explaining briefly the island's beliefs in the demigods of the forest. He traced the totems back to their Aztec source.

As he predicted, everyone in the room looked bored and had tuned out.

"Rubbish," Dr. Pritchaird responded when he'd finished. "Mindless rubbish. This is an educated island, with a major seat of learning. The people enjoy a high standard of living and are employed in some of the most advanced factories for the manufacture of electronic equipment in this part of the world. They don't put any stock in . . ."

Remember Iran. Think of the simplistic nature of the Shiite faith. Think of what they did with mobs and what they destroyed and how much they pushed back in the direction of the Middle Ages. . .

Sheriff thought all those things. But he didn't say them. Men like this Pritchaird would never learn. They would always see the world as a linear progression, knowledge always moving forward, human emotions always giving place to educated rationality, men preferring to live in light rather than darkness. Human nature didn't always work that way. Considering the human population as a whole, very few had the temperament to be scientists.

"What are *you* going to do, Sheriff?" Barton had broken into Pritchaird's tirade.

Sheriff lighted a Sobranie. He didn't smoke much now, but Barton and his cohorts made him uncomfortable. It wasn't pleasant being in a room full of assholes.

"I'm not going to do anything," Sheriff replied. "Dr. Pritchaird here has convinced me that there's no danger.

After all, these dolls are Aztec toys, and we're in the twentieth century.''

"Pack up," said Sheriff as he threw open the door of the hotel room.

"What the hell?" Roger demanded. He'd been lying diagonally across the bed in his underwear, absorbed in a Robert Ludlum adventure.

"Something's going to break, Roger."

"How do you know?"

"Signs. I feel it. I don't know how I know, but I do. And it won't be here in the city, either. The city's full of goddamn CIA people. Whatever is going to happen is going to happen in the interior. Jungle gear. We're going out *now.*"

Bewildered, Roger got his things together. His father sat on the edge of the bed, making telephone calls. First to Sheila Doles, the pilot. Then to Mr. Susaki. He wanted more information. He wanted to know *everything*.

The helicopter sped once more over the tops of the island jungle.

"You're nuts," said Sheila to the two men, but her tone of voice made it apparent she'd run into nuts before. "That's jungle down there. This is not going to be like pitching a tent in your goddamn backyard."

Sheriff and his son were silent.

"You don't even have a guide," Sheila went on. "Hell, a guide for this place doesn't even *exist.*"

Sheriff pointed over to the right—northward. "Easy," he said quickly, "over there."

The 'copter veered north, toward the radar installation belonging to the New Zealanders. A hundred yards south of it, she hovered over the forest. Both Sheriff and Roger were peering out through binoculars. To prevent the distortion of the glass, Sheriff had even pushed open the door of the helicopter.

Roger suddenly pointed, and Sheriff flicked the glasses that way. His son, and Michael, too, had caught something out of the corner of his eye. Movement along the perimeter of the clearing.

Just for a second. But it was gone now.

But whoever had been there—dark brown shapes against the mat of green and black foliage—had left something behind: tiny colorful shapes that were staked in the ground.

Eyes of the Sun.

Sheila answered a sudden squawk on the radio. A thickly accented voice demanded identification. After her response, the voice sounded again.

"You got it," said Sheila.

She replaced the speaker.

Roger and Sheriff had pulled away, having seen what they needed to see.

"Gotta get out of here, Sheriff. You got the NZ boys all upset. We're too close, interfering with their reception."

The bird whirled away over the jungle.

"Oh Jesus," the pilot sighed once more. "No wonder they all think Americans are crazy."

"We got to start somewhere," said Sheriff. "Here's as good as any. Listen," he said to Sheila, for he could see the worry in her eyes. "Tell me your operating frequency. I have a portable on me. If I need you, I'll radio you. You're not far away, less than a hundred miles. My transmitter can reach you, easy. If not there, then one of the installations. I'll get hold of you if I get in trouble."

"You're going to be in trouble the minute you hit that ground. This part of the island isn't for amateurs. Of course, maybe you two aren't amateurs . . ."

Sheriff didn't answer.

The helicopter was hovering directly above the ruins of the temple that Sheila had showed them just the day before. As Roger prepared his gear, Sheriff scanned the salted clearing beneath them. No strange shadows this time. He detected no movement in the forest.

"Ready," said Roger.

Serious for once. Good. Though Michael realized that this was the first time the kid had ever climbed down a flimsy rope ladder from the bay of a helicopter.

The 'copter was too large to land in the tiny temple grounds, without possibly damaging the blades against either the edge of the forest or the stone ruins.

Roger, perhaps to show that he wasn't really frightened at all, prepared to descend first. But Michael pushed him aside. "Cover me," he said quietly, as he waved and winked to Sheila.

Roger quietly pulled the Colt .45 from the pocket of his light jacket, and held it out of view of the pilot.

With his pack and his Remington .30-.30 strapped to his back, Sheriff clambered down the ladder through about ten meters of empty space, and then down into the ruins of the temple.

The last half-dozen meters of descent were inside the roofless temple. Even after long exposure to the sun, these old stained rock walls were damp and foul. There was a stink here too, a stink that Sheriff thought he recognized.

Sheriff looked around for a few moments, drawing out his revolver as well. Then with an abrupt gesture, he called Roger down from above.

Roger was even quicker in his descent. Not wanting to prolong unbalanced suspension high above a stone-floored temple, probably. Couldn't blame the kid.

Roger whistled when he hopped the last few feet from the ladder. Sheriff yelled, "Wait here," above the noise of the helicopter, poised directly overhead. Then he went out through an open doorway into the tiny temple ground. He waved to Sheila, and gave her the high sign. The ladder was drawn back into the helicopter hydraulically, and after a moment more, the machine sped away eastward, with a farewell flick of its tail blades.

Sheriff went back inside the temple.

Roger wasn't where he'd been told to wait.

With the noise of the helicopter suddenly gone, the place seemed ominously silent.

"Roger!" Sheriff called, quietly; for the temple was small.

"Here . . ." he heard a reply. Soft, strained.

Sheriff went that way. He passed a small aperture where a portion of a wall had toppled, and saw Roger in a small stone chamber on the other side.

Alone, but looking down at something.

Michael stepped over the rubble, and moved beside his son. Roger was standing in front of a hewn stone the size of a breakfast room table.

An altar.

On that altar, hidden in inner chamber of a ruined temple in the middle of one of the densest tropical forests on earth, lay four human hearts, so fresh that the blood that had spilled out of the filled arteries still lay in uncoagulated pools on the corrugated surface of the stone.

18

THE MACHETE IS ONE of the most dangerous of primitive weapons. Razor-sharp blades cut through the jungle growth with the ease of a hot knife through butter. At first it wasn't hard to swing their way through the foliage, but the constant repetition of the movement soon began to tax their strength. Untrained men would have been unable to hold up the long blade for the length of time it was taking them to make their way across the jungle.

But Michael and Roger Sheriff were in peak shape. The constant training on the Massachusetts farm had prepared them for just this kind of endurance. That had been its purpose. By taking shifts in leading the way, and therefore in suffering beneath the harder task, Michael and Roger were able to make time that would have astonished even jungle natives.

They'd searched the temple and clearing and found no one. Michael realized that he'd made a mistake by not landing in the clearing of the New Zealand operation. He had the feeling—it wasn't much more than that yet—that the next attack was going to be there.

As they moved, sweat soaking through their lightweight clothing, Michael and Roger talked about the assignment and what Michael had learned from Mr. Susaki and the meeting at the embassy. There were new facts to be taken into consideration, and Michael had the uneasy sense that they had a great deal to do with the trouble that had beset the island in the several months before their arrival. "Think about it," said Sheriff—for constant conversation was impossible—"and let me know if you come up with some ideas."

Now, in the field, there was no time for them to indulge in any of the fake competition of their private battles. Now, whether Michael liked it or not, Roger was his partner. Whether Roger liked it or not, Michael was in charge.

Information had to be shared quickly and efficiently. Roger was on a mission. The one thing an agent had to have was all the possible data. It had been one of the cornerstones of MIS. The function of those enormous computers in the basement of the Route 128 building was to feed a constant flow of information to the agents. With it, they had a chance. Without it, there was none.

If it hadn't been for the rank underbrush, the trek to the New Zealand installation wouldn't have taken more than an hour. If it hadn't been for the jungle, they might have reached the installation in time.

They didn't.

Even before they caught any glimpse of the clearing, the satellite dish arrays, or of the buildings, they captured the stinking odor in the air. Roger had never smelled it before, but he knew instantly what it was.

The stench of burning human flesh.

They slipped their packs off at the edge of the trees, took the safety off their rifles, and crept around the corner of the windowless building.

The first thing they saw was that the satellite dishes had been crippled—their narrow metal legs twisted, and some sort of small explosive, possibly a grenade, used to destroy the dish itself.

But in between the wrecked dishes was human wreckage.

A heap of smoking human corpses, black and twisted, the flesh tightened and charred around the bones, clothing in smoking tatters.

Michael moved closer, Roger behind—preferring to

watch out for attackers so that he wouldn't have to look at what the attackers had already accomplished.

Michael Sheriff picked up a scrap of metal and tossed it onto the heap of corpses. A vast buzzing swarm of flies clouded up, and then immediately settled back down again.

On the ground, the shorn grass was black with ants rampaging out of the forest toward the bodies.

"Their hearts have been torn out," said Michael Sheriff, peering into the heap and seeing the gaping cavity in the chest of each corpse.

Even the gasoline fire that had welded together and reduced this pile of perhaps fifteen or twenty dead men had not eradicated the evidence of that radical surgery.

Michael Sheriff looked over his shoulder at his son. Roger was alert, tense, looking this way and that.

Looking everywhere but at the corpses.

Too bad. Because there was worse to come.

Worse was on the other side of the clearing. Michael went that way, and motioned Roger to follow.

Might as well get this over with. The kid had signed up for MIS, he might as well see the payoff now.

There were only four women. All had been stripped naked before their torture. They'd been staked to the ground.

That is not to say that they'd been tied to stakes, but that the stakes had been driven through their hands.

Their legs had been broken to prevent their even attempting to crawl away.

It was impossible to tell if they'd been raped, though Sheriff supposed so. It was impossible to tell because there were now only boxy cavities where their sexual organs used to be.

The women's eyes were still wide open in shock.

Behind him, Michael heard Roger vomiting.

Good, he thought.

Those times Michael Sheriff had found himself approaching the attitude that human life had no meaning, no dignity, that death was a thing to be looked on without passion and without remorse, he had been ashamed for himself. In this line of work, dispassion was too easy a way out, too easy a response to the cruelty and horror that man can wreak on man. You had to revolt against it at the same time that you didn't let the horror weaken you. Not retreat in fear, but come out with a greater anger, fortified to the purpose of protecting other lives.

He didn't want his son to become one of those people who simply shrugged and walked on when he was confronted with cruelty. Nor could he allow his son to be incapacitated by a sight such as this. Roger couldn't allow himself to be paralyzed in the field, but Michael didn't want his son's heart to turn to stone either.

They'd talk about this later. Right now, though, he wanted to boy to feel. He wanted him to be revolted and upset and pissed off. He had to learn to keep on going. That was the next step.

"Can we do something for them?" Roger croaked miserably behind him.

"No, nothing. The scavengers are already at work. Even if we buried these four women, they'd be dug out of the ground again. If we cremate them, the smoke would alert those who did it. Besides, someone is bound to be on the way already—the communications were cut off, and that'll send the troops running."

Michael watched as Roger regained his composure. The kid was doing pretty well—well enough that there could be some relief to what he was going through. "Wait here," he ordered his son. "I'll check out the inside of the facility." After all he'd already seen, if there were more bodies inside, and if they were in this bad shape, Roger didn't need any more object lessons in what can happen on a battlefield.

A quick look around the New Zealand installation revealed no bodies, not even a sign of a struggle. The place was surreal to Michael as he went from room to room.

The facility was modern, even antiseptic—a space module landed in the midst of a primeval jungle.

When he was sure that there was no one lingering in the structure, he went back out to find his son waiting for him. Roger's eyes were carefully averted from the corpses.

Roger looked at his father. The boy's eyes were red and hard, his head averted from the four bloody forms on the grassy sward.

Too bad, thought Sheriff. Too bad it had to happen to the kid, and too bad his father had to be there to watch it happen.

"We've got another couple of hours of light," said Sheriff. "Whoever it was went back into the jungle this way."

He pointed into the mass of trees a few yards away.

"How can you tell?" demanded Roger, who evidently saw nothing at all different about that part of the tropical forest at the edge of the clearing.

Michael tried to remember he was a teacher. Roger was learning. Even if it meant going back through all the basics the boy should have known, Michael had to do it. He walked over to the point in the brush he had indicated. He wordlessly lifted up two branches that were still attached to a tree. They'd been broken. More than just broken, they were bent inward, toward the forest. Obviously, someone had moved in that direction recently. They had to have been moving fast in order to snap the green wood, and because the branches were more than a yard apart, there had to be more than just one person.

The two men plunged once more into the forest. With Sheriff in the lead, they quietly followed the trail of the butchers.

"How many are there?" asked Roger, then realized that was a foolish question. "About, I mean."

"Half a dozen," said Sheriff. "Can't be sure."

The sun was sinking toward the west. This deep beneath the canopy of trees, the air was already dim and cooling.

If they didn't catch up with the killers before dark it would be impossible to follow the trail.

Sheriff's speed through the forest became almost urgent. They proceeded with all possible quickness, and with all possible silence.

Roger felt their arrival at their destination before he actually saw it, for he caught the change in the covering of the floor. A hard covering, gleaming faintly beneath his feet, like broken slabs of concrete.

Hardened salt.

They'd returned to the temple.

Father and son were hidden in the edge of the forest. A chanting—in low masculine voices, in a language Michael couldn't identify—came from within the ruins.

No one was visible from where they stood. The broken blocks of the temple building were shining a faint blue in the deep tropical twilight.

Michael Sheriff motioned for Roger to follow him as he crept silently within the margin of trees to the other side of the temple.

The chanting grew louder as they proceeded, and Roger pointed—the gleam of an open flame, perhaps a torch, on a length of wall.

Whatever inhuman beasts had butchered the New Zealanders were now inside the temple.

Singing.

19

SHERIFF HESITATED a moment, weighing the choices.

He did not know how many men were inside the ruined temple, and he had no idea how they might be armed.

Certainly they were prepared to do battle, for there must have been *some* security at the New Zealand installation.

It appeared from the evidence of the trek through the forest that were no more than half a dozen; and the chanting voices suggested no greater number.

But it still might prove to be more, if some of those inside were silent, if the murderers moving through the jungle had been careful and experienced.

He was a man armed with a .45 revolver and a .30-.30 rifle.

His backup was a nineteen-year-old boy who had never been placed in such a situation as this.

His backup was *his son.*

Michael Sheriff entertained one fleeting picture in his mind: himself, tied up, watching as Roger's living heart was torn from his breast.

One fleeting second that picture played. Michael screamed in his mind, and then he flicked one finger at his son.

Let's go.

In the deepening twilight they crept toward the temple, the entrance away from the area where the singing sounded most strongly.

For a few moments the two men were exposed, naked, on the thick salt covering of the temple yard, but then they were hidden in the shadows of a tumbled wall.

Sheriff crept around the edge of the rubble. Roger followed as closely as he could, yet making certain he was not so near that he was likely to come in contact with his father.

No noise.

They knew where they were going. The room with the altar. More hearts were to be heaped onto the stone table into which canals had been dug to drain away the excess blood.

Not one word had been spoken by the two men since they'd reached the temple. Michael Sheriff had to trust to his son's instincts, his training, his intelligence, his cunning, and bravery in this enterprise.

They neared the fissure in the wall that gave entrance to the chamber of sacrifice.

The chanting was loud. The language had some familiar rhythms and vowel shapes, but Sheriff still didn't recognize it. It might have been an ancient language, or it might have been a modern language severely corrupted.

The rise and fall of the voices was hypnotic. The sky above them was fast deepening to black.

They were both on the same side of the fissure, crouching. It had already become obvious to Sheriff that all the murderers were inside the room. There'd been no indication of guards left outside the room, or of anyone watching. Why should anyone watch? The temple was in the middle of the jungle. The only habitation within twenty miles was the New Zealand facility—and everyone there was dead.

It was dark inside the temple. The fissure shone in a flickering golden light of the torch flames inside the room. Sheriff could smell some sort of crude oil being burned, maybe a kind of slag or pitch that was used for such primitive light sources.

All right, he said in his mind. *Deal with it, Roger.*

Without more thought, without counting one-two-three, without warning or noise of any sort, Michael Sheriff was suddenly on his feet, through the fissure and inside the room. He placed himself to the right of the entrance.

Before the men in the room had even noticed his intrusion, Roger was there as well, stationed on the left side of the door.

The butchers were just turning their heads toward Michael and Roger as they began to die.

It was while their rifles were blasting that Michael began to take in what was before him in the flickering, lurid light of the torches.

Five men.

Two wearing only loincloths, carrying machetes, with M-16 rifles slung over their shoulders. They were native Supartans. Or at least they had looked it for a second or two before their faces got blown away. The .30-.30's had special hot-load bullets in them. Unavailable to the public, even forbidden to civilian police departments in the States, the ammunition turned the simple hunting rifle into a weapon of incredible destruction. The bullets didn't just cut through a body and leave a clean wound. They were small bombs. They exploded on impact, sending minute but mortal shrapnel erupting outward. A normal bullet—if correctly aimed—could pierce a human chest, cutting out a path of destruction through a lung. A hot-loaded bullet meant you almost didn't have to aim. After it had done its work, there was no lung left at all.

Two others. Maybe natives too. But better clothed. In robes of some thin white material, heavily stained with blood and crushed vegetation. They wore gold ornaments on their wrists and their ears.

Then their garments, which had been stained with the dried encrusted blood of the New Zealanders, were stained afresh. With their own blood.

These two had stood at either end of the table.

Directly behind the table, wearing a white robe similar

to the others, but much less stained, was a short, masked figure.

His mask was of beaten gold, encrusted with gems.

He raised his hands in protest, and screamed out.

Roger jumped forward. A double-barreled blast of the .30-.30 exploded the mask and the head behind it.

"Behind you!" screamed Sheriff.

Not five men in the room, but six.

The sixth was cowering in a dark corner behind them, out of their sight. He leaped up out of the darkness with machete upraised.

Michael Sheriff blew off his hand.

The machete, still held in the grasp of the severed hand, flew away and scattered the mound of hearts on the table.

The sixth man tumbled forward at Roger's feet on the stone floor of the temple.

"Hey," said Roger, "I thought I was supposed to back *you* up."

The sixth man lay quiet on the floor of the temple, the robe of a dead priest wrapped around his wrist. The bandage was soaked through with blood and the man was slowly dying.

Michael had examined the other bodies. Nothing on them except the gold ornaments. The mask might have told them something, but that had been blown to fragments by the blast of Roger's gun. So was the head behind it. But the dark skin and the small stature of this highest of the priests suggested a native of Suparta.

Now came the part Michael didn't like—had never liked.

Torture.

Roger stood over the only survivor. "He's got another wound. Probably got it at the New Zealand installation. Bullet through the shoulder."

Michael peered down at the man. The small bullet

wound in his shoulder had been temporarily patched. "Does he speak English?" Sheriff asked.

"Yeah," said Roger. "He understands us."

The man was obviously trying to pretend that he did not, but Roger had detected the light of comprehension in his eyes.

"Too bad for him," said Michael. He really was sorry that the man knew the language, because that meant that Michael was going to have to make him talk.

No putting it off. The man was dying. Michael couldn't neglect his job just because he didn't want to have his son watch the things he was going to have to do.

There was only one way to make it bearable.

Turn it into another goddamn lesson.

"Information is the key, always," Sheriff began as he knelt beside the prisoner, turning the man so that the torch firelight shone on his face. "You have to collect information. That's your goal. Revenge isn't good enough. It's selfish and it makes you feel good for about twenty seconds. So you have to learn to make it slow, make it something that lingers. Two things are important: They have to stay alive, and they have to be able to talk."

Sheriff looked into his son's face, to see what he could read there. Nothing. Training to impassivity.

"There are two places that a man can't stand pain. One's a wound." Sheriff poked a finger at the shoulder bullet hole. The prisoner stiffened and his right arm flailed out.

Roger stepped on that hand with his jungle boot.

Bones crunched beneath and the man screamed.

"Eager beaver," said his father. "Take it easy. Then the other place is a man's nuts. The tenderest, most vulnerable part of a male body. Just a squeeze. A slight tap. That's all you need at first. Remind him what he's got, and remind him what he might lose."

Sheriff pushed the barrel of the rifle under the naked man's testicles, lifted them up, and let them drop again.

Then he pressed one of the balls in the tightened sac against the man's thigh.

The prisoner's response—despite the missing hand and the wound in his shoulder—was immediate.

"Now he's got a sense of how much he can be hurt. You do everything soft at first—you *don't*, by the way, crush the bones in their hands to start out with. You start out easy, because then they realize how far they've got to go."

Sheriff took two fingers, and pressed them on opposite sides of the shoulder wound. Mingled pus and blood oozed out. The man cried a strangled cry of agony at the pain.

"It's starting to fester," said Roger. "I guess that makes it hurt even more, right?"

"Sometimes a man wants to fight you, wants to prove that he can withstand anything that you do to him. They're fools. No one can withstand torture, really. The only way to get out of it is to die. If they let you."

The wounded man's eyes opened and he looked up into the shadowed faces of his captors. It was a look that Sheriff had seen before. Many times before. The look that said, *I'm going to die a painful, pointless death at your hands.* But now his son was seeing that strange, eloquent gaze for the first time.

Roger was attentive, hanging on his every word. Now and then glancing at the prisoner, his eyes probing those wounds the way Sheriff's fingers had.

Christ! What sort of father was he? Bringing his son halfway around the world to an abandoned rotting temple, where in the loneliness and darkness of the jungle night, he imparted the wisdom of the torturer?

20

ROGER WAS SPRAWLED on one of the beds in their hotel room. His mind was reeling. *Gonzo,* he told himself, *the whole thing is gonzo.* He tried to regain images of the Management Information Services headquarters in Massachusetts. It was so *clean.* It was efficient. It was simply and purely the home base for a multinational corporation, just the way commuters driving Route 128 thought it was. That was all, that was it.

The company had a man at the head of it called the Chairman. He had white hair, he was well educated and had impeccable taste. He was gentle and always kind—at least toward Roger, he had been. He had lots of money, and lots and lots of power. He had all the things that Roger wanted for himself.

Roger remembered wanting his father to take the Chairman's place. Get all that cash and all that influence and sit in a nice corner suite and watch the stupid fuckers commuting down on the highway. If you got that job, then you didn't have to worry about what went on in the field. You never had to think about what was going on in the heads of your agents—or your trainees.

You didn't have to watch men performing ritual murders and you did not have to smell the stench of dead bodies or see columns of ants spilling out of the gaping mouths of charred corpses. You didn't have to aim rifles and shoot to kill. None of that shit.

Roger tried to fight it off. He didn't want any of this

stuff running around in his head. But it was all there, the incredible amount of death, and its stupefying ugliness was rooted in his consciousness now. Oh hell, how could all that have happened?

It used to be that Roger spent all his time thinking about getting laid. Now all he thought about was turning people who are alive into people who are something else. Not alive.

Yeah, he had seen death before and he'd acknowledged his own capacity for violence before. He remembered the incident in the Boston Common—Christ, only a few weeks ago! That seemed so placid in comparison to what he'd just been through, taking out a couple of kids from Southie. That wasn't the same thing as firing a high-powered hunting rifle into a man's skull. That wasn't the same thing as sitting still and paying close attention while your dad crushed a man's testicles with the heel of his boot.

But no one had fooled him on this one. They'd all told him about it. His father, the Chairman, even Katrina had dropped hints. He had seen it in movies and he had heard all the stories from Vietnam veterans who hung around Reno. This was a rite of manhood he would have to go through. Yeah, right.

Avenging Stasia's death had been his first kill. That was sudden, hot blood. Hot blood was easy.

Shooting down the guys in the ruined temple was easy, too. Knowing what they'd done back at the New Zealand installation made pulling the trigger a sharp pleasure.

What was getting to him now was the torture. Crouching down on that stone floor in the jungle night, watching his father cause a man the worst pain that man had probably ever known. While Michael Sheriff kept up a little running commentary. This is how you do it, this works all the time, this works sometimes, if he still won't talk, then you try—

Right. His father had been so taken up with the lesson that he had almost forgotten the purpose of it all—to make the prisoner spill his guts. Finally the man had screamed—"Yes, yes!"

Both Michael and Roger had looked up, startled, and Roger—he was ashamed to admit this—had been disappointed.

The stories had come out, in halting English, slightly more fluid pidgin, but all with native terms mixed in that made following the tale difficult. The blood that filled up the man's mouth every few minutes didn't help matters either.

The man lived in the interior of the island, one of the isolated jungle villages that Sheila had pointed out to them from the helicopter. He and the others had been recruited by the priests of the great temple of the Sun God.

Recruited was not quite the right word.

They'd been sold by their parents many years before.

Didn't the authorities know and didn't the authorities free them?

There were no authorities in the interior. Only the priests of the Sun God. And his messengers.

Whose messengers?

The Sun God's. The Sun God's messengers who brought the commandment.

What commandment?

That the whites had to leave the island. The whites were infidels, they brought false gods, they desecrated the Sun God's temples, they brought false commandments to the people.

The man's voice was proud, even in his suffering. He may have been stolen or bought by the priests, but he had learned to love and be proud of that bondage. When his testicles were swollen to three times their normal size, the story did not change or expand.

"That's all he knows," his father had said, and put a bullet into the prisoner's brain.

The smell of the spent powder flared in Roger's nostrils, stronger than the prisoner's blood and shit, and he opened his mouth to protest.

Michael Sheriff had looked at him, as if to say, *I had to kill him.*

But Roger had only wanted to keep the man alive so that the lesson in torture could continue.

Is that what came from working with MIS, finding out the darkest parts of yourself, those parts that you'd never discover if there hadn't been this catalyst, this unholy job? That prisoner had been like a cadaver donated to science—Michael Sheriff was the professor of anatomy and Roger the eager medical student. They'd cut him up. In this case, even though the corpse wasn't really dead, Roger had been anxious to experiment.

He felt ashamed of that now. He felt something terrible was going on inside himself. He thought that he was turning into something he had no control over. He could never, ever, admit this to his father—oh no, he could never say, "Yeah, well, Dad, the torture bit isn't so bad. Next time the business comes up, why don't you let me take a stab at it . . ."

Because despite his shame and his anger, he wanted it.

A knock at the door interrupted Roger's thoughts. He got up and answered it. Sheila Doles came in, for the first time since they'd met her, dressed in something other than jeans. Just a dozen hours before, she'd answered their radio summons and picked them up, shortly after midnight, from the site of the ruined temple.

Michael Sheriff, who'd been sitting in a chair by the window studying a map of the island, nodded. "Thanks for coming over."

Sheila's move into the room was hesitant.

"Something's going on," she said. "That New Zealand installation—"

"What did you hear?" Sheriff asked quickly.

"Nothing, that's what strange. They're operating on secret frequencies. But there's activity, I can tell you that. Did you . . ."

Sheriff shook his head. He wasn't saying *no*, he was saying *I can't talk about it*.

Roger wondered about all this. His father was the one always going on about secrecy, maintaining cover at all costs, never trust anybody, always be on your guard. But with this woman, he was almost casual. She knew they weren't a college professor and his student assistant doing work on comparative religion, and though Michael hadn't admitted that to her outright, he wasn't doing a hell of a lot in the other direction either.

It was apparent from his attitude toward her that Michael Sheriff trusted Sheila Doles.

"I need your help," he said.

"With what?" she asked uncertainly, and glanced at Roger.

Michael came over to the small desk in the corner of the room, spread out the map of Suparta, and then motioned over both Roger and Sheila.

"I've been studying this, and there's something wrong."

They looked at the map. It showed the island. The cities on the eastern coast, the villages and industrial centers on the northern shore, the tiny villages with outlandish native names scattered through the interior, the observation installations, the various roads and streams through the rain forest.

"No," she said, "that map is accurate. Listen, I fly over this goddamn island five times a week, at *least*—"

"That's it," Sheriff said quickly. "You *fly* over it. Why haven't we been using these goddamn roads?"

He pointed out the mesh of fine lines that crisscrossed the island, connecting the interior villages.

Sheila laughed. "I'll tell you why. You got a couple of four-wheel-drive vehicles you want destroyed? This is a historical map. Those are the ancient roads. They haven't been kept up in a hundred years, I bet. Just cut blocks of stone through the forest. They can't even be used for transport, and there are only a couple of places you can see them from the air—and even then you have to know what you're looking for.''

"Pack animals?" asked Sheriff.

"Not in Suparta. I think there's a pet water buffalo up at the university, but that's the only big animal on the island. Everything was killed off, or died off, or is so deep in the jungle that nobody even knows it's there. Listen," she said, drawing her finger along the features of the map. "This is modern Suparta. Suparta is Pato Lako and Satuka, the two cities, and it's the highway that connects them. It's these factories and villages up here. It's this little string of resort hotels on the south coast. The rest is jungle, jungle, jungle, and about five people who are too stupid to move to the coast. That's Suparta, guys.''

"Five people in the interior?"

"Twenty, thirty thousand tops," she estimated. "But they're all scattered. It's hard to count. Suparta doesn't have an official census. So they can estimate high for PR's sake. Sometimes the people from the interior send their kids to the coast to get educated, and sometimes the kids stay—but most of the time they go back and nobody ever hears from them again. The people on the coast think the interior people are hillbillies. The people in the interior think the coastal people are degenerates. Sound familiar?"

Sheriff nodded, distracted. "Same thing as with the installations . . ."

"What?" Sheila asked quickly. It was evident she *knew* something had happened at the New Zealand post, though she didn't know what exactly. She also suspected that Michael and Roger had had something to do with it.

"It's a matter of information," said Sheriff. Roger heard that same statement the night before, in a different context. It was the preamble to the lesson in torture. "The data I got on those installations. It was enough to make sense. But the problem was, it wasn't *all* the data. We got enough background on this island to have everything make sense—*superficial* sense—but goddamn it, nobody went beyond that. They've put us on this island without that and the fucking computers didn't do their job. They didn't *see.* ''

Sheila had taken a couple of steps back. She wasn't scared, but she was listening intently—as if now convinced nobody was going to spill to her, but they were going to permit her to figure the situation out. She looked as if she was going to be pretty good at it.

Michael picked up the telephone. He barked orders into it, demanding two transoceanic calls be placed immediately: one to a town on the outskirts of Boston, the other to the United Nations.

21

ALL ROGER WANTED was to make believe the world was a calm and normal place. He had not seen all that back in the jungle. His father was not blathering about computer breakdowns over transoceanic telephone lines. He had not enjoyed watching a man tortured to death. None of it.

Roger left the hotel room and wandered down to the lobby. Michael had barely acknowledged his departure. He stood outside the entrance to the bank of elevators where he'd just been deposited and saw the bar across the way. That was appealing. But there was another, even better, thought. He went to the house telephone and picked up the receiver. When the operator answered he said, "Suite 1500, please."

Fifteen minutes later he had both Lin Tao and a tall drink in his hand. He had been surprised that her suite was so much larger than his room. He'd come to expect that MIS always took the best in everything. But Lin Tao's spread was at least twice the size of the Sheriffs' accommodations.

She was dressed differently this time. Now her clothing accentuated her racial identity. The tight dress of dark blue raw silk had a mandarin collar and long slits in the skirt. Roger got tantalizing glimpses of thigh as Lin Tao made her way toward the couch where he sat.

"You are becoming an afternoon habit. A pleasant one." She toasted him with her glass. He played along and let his own touch hers softly, with a musical clink.

They each took a sip of drink. Roger forced himself to relax. "I never let you say a thing about yourself," he said. "I did all the talking. Who are you? I mean, really? I want to know." *Take my mind away from here. What I've seen. What I've done.*

She shrugged. "I am a Chinese with a British passport."

He looked surprised by that.

"You must understand," she explained, "the Chinese have many legal nationalities. We are spread all over Asia, we have always been. We are a trading people. Every port on the Pacific and most on the Indian Ocean has a Chinese colony. Of course, today, with the Communists in charge of the mainland and the Nationalists restricted to Taiwan, well, many of us have taken other papers. Especially British. Those of us, like myself, who grew up in Hong Kong, or trace our families back to the Crown Colony, have been British subjects for centuries. It's very common in Asia for us to introduce ourselves that way, 'Chinese, with a British passport,' or a Thai or Malaysian passport."

"How did you get to this country?"

"My father is the agent for a large conglomerate in Hong Kong. He was assigned here. I came with him about ten years ago. Suparta is pleasant enough."

"Pleasant enough." Roger looked around the huge suite again. "What does he trade in to afford this?"

Lin Tao appeared amused by Roger's enthusiasm. "My father is a broker. He and his conglomerate find many things to trade. Hong Kong merchants are very seldom poor, Roger. We are the traders of the East in the way that the Venetians were the great traders of medieval and Renaissance Europe."

Roger drank more of his scotch and let his eyes wander appreciatively around the room again. The suite was obviously rented for more than a package-tour stopover. There were indications that the stuff on the walls, and probably the furniture as well, were Lin Tao's own. It certainly didn't read as hotel furnishing.

Lin Tao shifted on the couch beside him. She moved closer to him with that movement, close enough that he could smell that same odor that he'd waked to earlier in the day.

Her hand slid toward his neck. A finger traced an imaginery line on his skin, sending little bumps up and down his flesh. He stiffened. A nice little ordinary fuck with a nice extraordinary lady. That was just what he needed. He knew he was going to get it.

He looked into Lin Tao's eyes and for the first time saw how much rounder they appeared to be than American women's. That was strange. Asians were supposed to be slant-eyed, that was the stereotype. And there was a way in which the lids on Lin Tao were more severely arced than with Caucasians. But the eyes themselves, the roundness of the brown center, wasn't slanted in any way.

Impulsively he leaned over and put his lips on first her left eye and then her right. It had been the first tender urge he'd felt. He had wanted to give into it.

She smiled. "The ardor of young men is so strange, it has so many forms." Then she stood, holding out her hand with an unmistakable invitation for him to join her in the other room. He put down his drink and stood to follow.

She let go of him only when they'd gotten to the enormous bed. There she spread herself on the silk cover. It was a bright red, a Chinese red, he realized. It set off the blue of her dress and the almond color of her skin.

She arranged her body in an unmistakable fashion, allowing—forcing?—her slit dress up her legs till the opening on one side was actually up to her waist. Her hands moved behind her neck and caressed her long hair. She lifted it up and let it fall down over her face.

He was hypnotized by her performance. Her hands now moved down and slowly cupped her breasts. He was hard already. The confinement of his pants was suddenly unbearable. ''Get undressed,'' she said.

He stripped quickly. The fact she didn't take off her own clothes simply didn't register with him. She was already telegraphing such sexual heat that he didn't even think that her being clothed was in any way a lack of sexual interest or intent.

Naked, his erection spearing the air, he didn't have time to be embarrassed. He moved onto the bed. His knees and his lower legs pressed against the silk cover. The cool slick surface was an erotic shock. He moved up to bring his knees to either side of her hips.

She still smiled. Now a hand came and tenderly grabbed hold of his balls. She used them as a hold to motion him farther up the bed. He knew what she wanted to do and he had no intention of stopping her. He followed her lead, watching his hard cock as it led the way, right into her waiting lips.

He closed his eyes with the intense explosion of sensation that came over him when her wet lips engulfed him. He tried to be romantic. *This is something nice she's doing for you*, he told himself. He fought the urge to push his erection into her mouth. There was a part of him that wanted to gag her, but he allowed only the softest undulations to ripple through his hips.

Her hands left his testicles, moved behind and took hold of his buttocks, kneading them. She wasn't trying to increase his motions. She obviously enjoyed having that control herself. Her mouth moved at her own speed as it slid up, then down his shaft. Each of the minute retreats left a wet slick on the suddenly naked skin of his cock that felt cool, even in the warm tropical air.

His eyes were closed now as he fought off the building orgasm. Lin Tao was obviously enjoying her ministrations. He was certainly having his own good time. He wanted it to last forever.

Reaching out, Roger found the wall behind the bed, slumped forward and rested against it. The new position created an even better angle for her mouth. He could hear slight sucking noises now, wet sounds that kept time with the pulsing of her mouth.

Roger couldn't take it anymore. He pulled himself back, away from her, and moved downward so the whole of his body could lie atop her. Looking down, he saw Lin was still smiling. Her smallness beneath him made him feel big, powerful. His erection jammed up into the folds of her dress, his thighs felt that cool touch of the silk cover. They kissed, tongues dancing. There was more wetness, wetness he could taste now.

He couldn't stop his pelvic movements. Roger *had* to thrust. His cock caught on her dress, bending his erection with slight pain. Enough! He rolled off Lin. He didn't have to say a word, though, as she tore the dress over her head in a quick motion. There were no other garments beneath it.

That smile remained. Roger didn't have time to move before Lin had climbed on top of him. Her hand pressed down on his chest and her legs straddled him. With one hand, she reached down to grab hold of his cock and forced it upward till it was perpendicular to his body. Another little stab of pain hit him. But it was soon overwhelmed by the hot drowning feeling of her embracing the entire length of him.

Lin clenched her vaginal muscles around his sex, then leaned over, letting her small, perfect breasts brush against his chest hair again and again. She kissed him, her tongue invading his mouth once more.

Now it was Roger's hands on her ass, clutching even harder than she had at him, trying to get deeper inside her—impossible, for their pubic hair was already meshed together. He moved side to side, hoping to get a more intense sensation, something that would feel even better than what was already happening to him.

At some point the sheer perfection of it all caught him: A beautiful Chinese woman was sitting on his cock, while the finest silk massaged his ass and back. With each breath, he scented the most exquisite and expensive perfume. His erection was enormous, bigger than all the rest of him, it was sheathed in warm, wet forbidden flesh and it felt . . .

Torturous spasms racked through his body, expanding outward from his crotch to seize control of every muscle and nerve ending. He arced himself upward, lifting her as he did. As they kissed, he sucked on her tongue, maddened with some primal thought that he had to do it now, he *had* to because he was drowning her with everything that was flowing out of his cock into her. She had to be drowning . . .

Then he collapsed back onto the silk, all the energy drained from him. He looked up at her with his mouth open, idly slack. He was unable to even consider closing it. Sweat poured off his forehead. And hers as well, he could see that. The elegant black hair was plastered to her skin at the line of her forehead.

She let him rest. After a short while she shifted slightly and his spent penis slipped out of her and flopped, exhausted, onto his belly. She moved to his side, leaving one leg rolling over his hips. "As I said," she teased, "the ardor of youth."

In a while they showered, lathering each other friskily. Roger was vaguely aware of a desire to get it on again. He loved the feeling of her soaping him up and he felt himself freed by her uninhibited manner.

They dried off and he wrapped his towel around his waist. Lin Tao retrieved a silk dressing gown for herself. She didn't bother to tie the belt, but let it float. The gown flapped open to reveal the dark smooth hair of her sex as they walked back into the bedroom.

Roger sprawled on the bed again.

"Your towel is too damp," Lin protested. "It will ruin my spread." She laughed and took it off him, leaving him naked again. "That's fine. Just stay there with that foolish smile on your face. I'll get you a new drink."

When Lin Tao returned in a few minutes, the smile

was gone. Roger was staring straight ahead at the wall, an expression of dread and shock on his face.

"Is something wrong?"

"What's that?" He pointed across the room to the decoration, that in his lust, he hadn't noticed.

Lin Tao carefully put his glass on the bedside table. Speaking with apparent casualness, she replied, "It's simply a local artifact. A mask. My father trades in them. I thought that one was particularly . . . interesting, so I kept it for myself."

The visor was of beaten metal; it appeared to be silver. It was all of a single piece with openings for a mouth and two round eyes. It wasn't the mask that Roger had seen in the temple—that had been gold, with a more masculine appearance. But the masks were indubitably of the same type and manufacture.

Even when I want to run off for a good time, this shit's going to come back and haunt me. There is no end to it . . .

"I haven't seen them in the markets," Roger said. That was true. Nor had there been anything like it in any of the native restaurants that were supposedly so authentic in their decor.

"The people in the cities don't keep the old gods." Lin Tao's voice was strangely cold now. "These are only found in the interior. Or so I'm told."

"But no one goes there," Roger protested.

"You have to understand the ways of the Chinese— especially the Hong Kong Chinese. We go anywhere to make a profit." Lin Tao watched Roger intently. Then she seemed to soften a bit. "Of course, you're studying the ancient religions. You know about the gods and demons, more than other people do. Perhaps you recognize Mahal'ak, the Goddess of the Moon."

Roger nodded, covering his shock as he remembered that even in this woman's bedroom he had to keep his cover. "Yeah, I do."

He sat up and swung his legs over the edge of the bed.

He grabbed his drink and took a swig of it. "I guess I'd better be going. My . . . professor will be wondering where I am." His cover was nearly blown. That one remark—he'd nearly said my *father*—would have ruined the whole thing. Training! Remember your training and get it through your thick skull that you can't escape from your own chosen place in the world. Not even in the arms of a beautiful woman.

He stood up and mechanically recovered his slacks and the rest of his outfit. He put them on quickly, not looking at Lin Tao. That was a mistake—because it meant he didn't see the calculating, mistrustful expression she wore.

22

THE CHAIRMAN PUT DOWN the telephone receiver and leaned back in his office chair. He looked blankly out of the narrow windows. Few people ever saw him in this mood. It only came over him when the worst was happening. There was nothing to be gained by allowing either his staff or his clients to see him in this condition. Nothing at all, and much might be lost.

The computers had failed.

Michael Sheriff's angry accusations over the telephone had been intensified because of Roger's presence in Suparta. The Chairman knew that. He had filtered that emotional response as he had listened carefully to what Michael had told him of the inadequacy of the MIS preparation.

The Chairman had sent his two operatives into the field without accurate or sufficient information.

The MIS computers were the most advanced in the world, and had established the state-of-the-art benchmark for artificial intelligence. There was absolutely nothing wrong with them. Nothing at all. They had not malfunctioned. But they had one intrinsic flaw: They could only deal with the data that was entered into them by human beings. The human beings hadn't seen and the computers couldn't postulate from nothing. It was that grotesquely simple.

Given the data they'd been fed, the computers had reported a scenario that made perfect sense to the Chair-

man, to Sheriff, and to anyone else who would ever investigate the situation in Suparta. There were high-
technology installations of critical importance to the
American government and many of its allies. Any enemy, given the situation that had been reported in Suparta, would have been going after those installations as a
means of weakening the Western allies, and of obtaining
valuable technology. Sheriff had been sent in expecting
to find what the incompetent CIA had missed—an Eastern bloc organization that was out to destroy Western
communications, and perhaps also, at the same time, to
foment a leftwing revolution on the geographically strategic island.

That scenario was no longer realistic. The data were
incomplete, the computations and conclusions insuffi-
cient and probably misleading. What were Michael and
Roger Sheriff looking for? A needle in a haystack. A
force moving in an unseen and unacknowledged society
that inhabited the interior of Suparta.

The sun-worshipping priests had originally been
thought a subterfuge. But were they? The data had concluded that the old religions had been superseded by the
various and strong proselytizing Western and Asian
creeds. But had they been? Suparta was supposed to enjoy a stable government. It did, but only along the coast.

Suparta had the potential to erupt just as Iran had.
Then, operatives had seen the Shah and his glorious,
forward-moving capital—not the hordes of religious fanatics in the interior. Vietnam: We saw the orderly (if
corrupt) government and its pledges of democracy, not
the swarm of rebels in the interior who were constantly
growing in strength and anger and purpose. China: We
saw the Nationalists and their chic cities, Shanghai and
Nanking, not the true believers on the Long March gathering strength for themselves, sapping it from the central
government.

Now, Suparta. We saw high-tech industries being at-
tacked and assumed high-tech motives. We simply didn't

see those thirty thousand people in the interior of the island—and thirty thousand people have raised revolts against larger and sturdier nations than Suparta.

Michael and Roger were in Suparta with the cover of studying the native religions. Ambassador Tufalo had caved in to Sheriff's demanding questions and had given him a glimmer of an idea how to proceed with his investigations. They were truly going to be the researches of a highly trained academic. The cover would have to become reality.

The Chairman looked over the room and out the window to observe the late-night traffic on Route 128. Dark shapes of trucks, automobile lights white in one direction, dim and red in the other. His most accomplished operative was in the field with only the support of his untried adolescent son.

It was the Chairman's responsibility. He went back over the situation in his head. He would never, he knew, admit this to a soul, but he was worried, frightened, that he had made a tactical error that might lead to the death of his most trusted and even beloved subordinate. If that happened, he would never forgive himself. Something inside him would die.

23

THE VILLAGE OF Trali was a stark contrast to the opulent
wonders of Pato Lako and the elegance of the capital,
Satuka. It was composed of a few thatched-roof huts,
none of them with walls. The warm tropical climate of
the island didn't require anything except some barrier to
keep the rainy season's precipitation off the heads of
those sleeping beneath. Naked screeching children ran
around, playing. The adult residents moved more slowly,
smiling and happy. Roger was sorely disappointed when
he finally saw native women with naked breasts. Some
did have the picture-perfect breasts of his dreams, but
most hung low and flat from the effects of nursing and
old age.

But then, Roger and his father were in a different scene
themselves. The tourists' outfits they'd worn for the first
few days in the country had been replaced by khaki clothing and tough boots that would even stand up to a jungle
like the one that surrounded Trali.

When Michael had thrown the outfits at Roger, the son
had wondered what all this was about. Why did they need
to put on the drab slacks and shirts? But as soon as he'd
seen himself in the mirror and then turned and looked at
his father, he'd understood. They were now in uniform:
unmistakably military in appearance and purpose.

They had bowie knives strapped on their belts. They
were still carrying the Remington .30-.30 rifles, and
bands of spare hot-load ammunition were attached to

belts that crossed their chests and then wove around their waists. They each had a holster with a Karlsrupa automatic pistol; the Swedish handgun was standard MIS issue. As with everything else MIS bought, it was simply the best available. Their hats were not for fashion shows, but were sturdy and thick for protection against the blistering sun. In the packs they carried camouflage makeup—they would smear it beneath their eyes to cut the glare that might interfere with their vision, and to make certain their white skin wasn't obvious in the dense, dark rain forest foliage.

It was all strange to Roger. The men going into the field. They had dehydrated rations in their packs to supplement any food they could scavenge. They were armed to the teeth and wore enough ammunition to stand off an army. They were *not* playing any games. It was no longer a question of finding the answer to a puzzle in the Honolulu airport. The idea of fucking a woman on the white beaches of the island was as far away as the house in Sudbury. They were in the field and there was immediate and real danger. They were going up against a group that killed every white man they came across. Roger was scared shitless.

He could fucking *die*.

Michael had walked up to the one large hut in the village. Sheila accompanied him, dressed in the same sort of outfit as the two Sheriffs. Then Michael squatted in front of an ancient-looking man, while Roger stood back and to the side. Sheila stood even farther back, only close enough to be able to translate the Supartan language.

The older Sheriff had cross-examined Ambassador Tufalo by telephone. Roger had listened to at least the beginning of his father's tirade against the diplomat. The language and the tone that Michael had used left no room for equivocation. There had been answers, hurried lessons had been learned. Michael Sheriff hadn't wanted any more bullshit about modern Suparta. He wanted to know the old ways, the proper manner of speaking to an elder, the manner of speech and tone that would communicate great respect.

These were things that in another situation—as, for instance, in preparation for an assignment in Leikawa a year earlier—Michael would have studied at his leisure, and at home in Sudbury. Now he had to get them by transoceanic communication in a single hour. But he still had to get them *right*.

Roger held his breath while he watched his father. He gripped his rifle hard, conscious that his knuckles were turning white from the tension and strain. Sitting in front of Michael was an extraordinarily old-looking man. His skin was wrinkled beyond Roger's belief. His eyes were barely slits, and at first Roger had thought him actually blind. But then Roger caught the intelligence between those narrow lids.

Behind the old man stood a male who looked to be about Roger's age. He was the village elder's grandson, Roger assumed. He wore the same loincloth as the older guy; the five-inch strip of cloth was gathered by a rope belt at the waist. It went down underneath his crotch and the long, attached flap dangled as far down as his knees. He had a spear longer than he was tall, and a knife, naked of any sheath, was attached to the rope belt. And, like his grandfather, he was barefoot.

The grandson stared at Roger. Roger wanted to interpret this as a sign of respect for the older men. But another realization seized him.

Jesus. They're cannibals.

Michael was playing with a stick in the sand before him, not looking up, intent on his scribbling, as though waiting for permission to speak. The old man finally uttered something to him in a guttural language.

Sheila translated, "He is not used to people visiting here from the cities. Particularly not white people."

"Tell him I am honored to do so," Michael said, still not looking up, still avoiding the older man's eyes.

The old man spoke again.

"He wants to know what you want here. He and his people have had enough of the missionaries."

"I am not a missionary. I am a warrior."

He even sounds like it, Roger thought as Sheila translated the words. This was a part of his father he'd never seen.

"Who am I, he asks, and who is the youngster?"

"You are my woman, a kept woman—don't fuck it up, Sheila—and that is my son, a worthless adolescent. Don't say a word, Roger."

All that spoken in the same tone, so that the old man would not perceive the lies through Sheriff's voice.

Sheila translated again.

"He asks again why you are here."

Michael began to recite a version of the stories of ancient ways that he had learned from Tufalo, taking a long shot. "I am from the other part of the world where the sun-priests came from. I respect the old ways. I know there is difficulty here now with the new sun-priests."

As Sheila went into the Supartan language Roger could see the old man and the grandson stiffen with anger.

"What concern is it of yours that there would be trouble with the sun-priests?" the grandson broke in. The difference in language was obviously no problem to him, and he'd understood every word that Sheriff had said. Roger was only a little surprised this young man knew English—he'd been told that some of the inhabitants of the interior ventured out to the coastal schools.

Michael hesitated, as if wondering if the grandson's speech were a breach of etiquette that would anger the old man. He now repeated himself to the old man in the guttural tongue. The leader nodded to Michael, and from this point on the grandson translated. But Sheila moved to the side, and by a slight inclination of her head, she let Michael know whether the grandson's translations were accurate. They were.

"There is much that is going on in Suparta," Sheriff began. "Many changes. Things are different than they were even a year ago. Some of the old ways are reappearing, but in forms I don't believe you agree with.''

This was the gamble. That this one village and this one elder could be a key to the Supartan problem. Trali was supposed to be the village with the most carefully maintained traditions of the old religions—including the sense of warrior's honor and noble warfare. This old man probably still told stories of the islanders' repulsion of the Dutch who attempted to settle the island late in the eighteenth century.

The old man listened to his grandson and then seemed to come alive. He sat straighter, as though an inbred nobility were coming to the surface once more. He nodded and spoke. The grandson translated:

''The old ways are constantly changing. Other ways, other people, other religions have always built their huts in this land. Our religion has stayed with us because it takes a little of all, and does not fight. Some of our old ways are ways of the world. My grandfather understands that,'' said the young man. Then he paused and added, ''But some are . . . not good.''

''I would like for you and your grandson to join my boy and me,'' said Sheriff. ''To discover the false sun-priests.''

Another chance. Because maybe the rites that had been performed on the New Zealanders were the *real* rites of the Supartan sun-priests. And maybe, just maybe, this old man was at the head of the whole goddamn thing. And maybe neither Michael Sheriff, nor Roger, nor Sheila would ever again lie on the Supartan beaches. Instead, their hearts might be stacked up with the others on that evil-smelling altar at the center of the ruined temple deep in the jungle.

But the old man nodded. So there *were* false sun-priests, and the old man was neither in league nor sympathy with them.

''The false priests,'' said the grandson, ''say we must bring back the oldest ways. They do not respect the ways of the world and the way of the gods. My grandfather is an old man, but he understands that we must move with the times.''

Christ, thought Roger, sweat pouring down his back, *I'll never complain about a heavy course load again.* He'd begun thinking how much he'd like to be back at Breslauer where the library was air conditioned, and where there were no cannibals or heart-butchers, and where he wasn't continually on edge thinking that he might be shot up or carved out or pierced through any minute.

"I am part of the new times," Roger's father said. "I honor the old times. Can we work together?"

The elder listened to his grandson translate. He considered Michael's proposal. He spoke. The grandson said: "Maybe. But the boy is too young."

The grandson looked into Roger's eyes. Despite the fact that his cheeks were already flushed with heat and anxiety, Roger felt that he blushed.

Michael Sheriff looked back at his son. Nineteen. Yes, he should be too young. But not at this time, there was no option. "He has been trained. He has skills."

"He is too young," said the grandson, this time not waiting for the old man to speak. The grandson himself was probably not more than twenty.

"Is there some way . . . ?"

The young man smiled. He crossed his spear arm over his chest. The weapon now rested at an angle in the dirt. "He can fight against me."

"He will," Michael replied without hesitation.

24

AND NOW A nightmare.

Roger couldn't believe what was happening to him. He was standing in the middle of a crowd of people, wearing nothing but the same kind of loincloth that the other men had. In one hand was a knife, in the other a spear. The ground had been marked off in a large circle. He was about to start a fight to the death with Butolo, the grandson of the elder who had issued the challenge.

Except for one thing: He was under strict orders not to let Butolo die. The fucking native guy might kill him, but Roger was not allowed to kill his opponent.

Michael Sheriff had told Roger over and over again not to do it. If Roger won, then Butolo, according to the old ways of the island, would be his best friend. Butolo *could* possibly *consider* the same option if he won. But it was only an option. He would have every right to murder Roger right there in front of his father.

That was the kicker. Because Roger knew that Michael Sheriff, a man obsessed with his mission, just might let that happen. So this was his real initiation into the ways of Management Information Services. To stand nearly naked with a spear and a knife and face an opponent from out of the dark ages—and do it in front of your father who might just stand by and watch as this asshole punctured your body with a triangular piece of sharpened steel.

From reality to fantasy and then into nightmare.

He remembered back to the time, only a few hours

162

earlier, when his hands had been gripping the rifle so hard his muscles grew inflexible and tired. Now they had to relax as they held on tightly to the stock of the spear. This was not a time for nervousness. This was one of those moments his father had drilled him for: a peak performance time. Life or death was resting on his mind and his body and his ability to integrate the two of them.

Please, God . . .

Well, Roger supposed a little prayer wasn't going to hurt about now. Off to the side a gong sounded—a grating metallic noise. Butolo was crouching, his arms spread apart, his legs as well. He was moving from his side of the circle toward Roger.

I would much rather be taking care of a bunch of punks in the Boston Common, Roger thought.

Butolo didn't have Roger's hard muscles, at least not so obviously. Like most South Pacific men, there was a covering of soft flesh over his, and no sharp or heavily defined lines. But Roger wasn't deceived by Butolo's appearance of softness, not in the least. He had also observed the fluidity with which Butolo moved. That took practice, and it sure spoke loudly enough of the man's years of training.

Roger took his own stance and the two young men began to circle one another. Each held a knife in his right hand and a spear in his left. Deadly weapons, highly trained warriors.

Nightmare.

Roger remembered his father's speech about football players getting slapped on the ass so their inhibitions didn't interfere with their performance on the field. It hit home right now because his loincloth offered absolutely no protection. Until a short while ago Roger's concern about being nude in front of a crowd might have interrupted his concentration. The idea that his balls might fall out of the loose covering would have made him very nervous. Now? He could care less. He just wanted to get out of this shit alive, and without hurting his opponent.

What kind of shit was that? Not only keep himself
alive, he had to take care of this obviously skilled man on
the opposite side of the circle as well? It was, Roger realized, the kind of situation he was going to find himself in
time after time in the future—if there was a future. This
was the way it was going to be with MIS. Now he understood why the goddamn fees were so high. MIS—

*Forget MIS. Forget your father. Forget your balls
hanging out in the open, forget your fear. You are an MIS
operative and you should be ready for this at any and all
times. You are in combat. You are in the field. You have
an assignment.*

Adrenaline or fear pushed Roger's mind into over-
drive. With a blinding clarity of purpose and perception,
Roger registered the current situation, analyzed, planned
for the next move, anticipated his opponent's next move,
formed contingencies—just like the goddamn MIS computers. Nothing was going to interfere with that concentration.

Suddenly he was The Shield's son.

Roger had to know his enemy's defenses. He parried,
first to the left and then to the right, only to test Butolo's
reactions. Good, he was very good. He handled himself
as quickly as Roger, even though he was overtly surprised that the younger man had made the first moves,
and had made wise ones, not overextending himself, not
going too far.

Butolo lost his confident smile after that maneuver.
Roger was pleased; his opponent was taking him seriously. Now only motion and movement concerned
Roger. He was oblivious to the ground beneath his bare
feet, his meager loincloth. He became one with the spear
and the knife.

Roger had to keep remembering that he wasn't supposed to kill this man. What was he supposed to do when
it came down to the choice between killing Butolo and
letting himself die, though? Did his father expect him to

die for the sake of the mission? Probably. Roger just had
to make sure it didn't come down to that.

Then there was a sudden, crackling bolt in his mind as
he realized that he was liking this. No, loving it. He even
fleetingly wondered if he would get an erection. He recalled the excitement of the fight on the Common. It
hadn't been really sexual, but he knew it was close,
something similar.

But it didn't matter now because he wouldn't care if he
did. He was aware only of his opponent. He could see
only Butolo's body and his eyes and they continued their
careful stocktaking.

There was a flashing move on Butolo's right. The attack came so fast that Roger nearly missed it—but only
nearly. He was *not* going to go down. He was *not* going
to fuck up. He was not going to lose this one, *no way.*

Another parry to his left brought a searing pain, but
Roger dismissed it. He had assimilated everything his father had ever told him about the human mind's ability to
control pain. And he ignored the sticky liquid spilling
down his forearm toward his wrist.

Then he moved, but in a way that Butolo had never
imagined and was not prepared to defend against. Butolo
was looking for the wounding, expecting the kill. But
Roger was only looking to incapacitate. Instead of the
head of the spear lunging toward Butolo's body, it went
toward the earth, between the open space of his legs.

While Butolo's knife was diving toward Roger with a
movement that would have assured instant death, Roger's spear was churning and twisting. Butolo suddenly
found himself flying through the air. He fell heavily on
his back, a noise of air leaving his lungs nearly as loud as
a real groan would have been.

In less than two seconds, Roger dove onto his opponent using his weight to knock out of Butolo what little
air remained in his lungs. Thus pinned by Roger, Butolo
could neither move his extremities, nor catch enough
breath to throw him off.

In one incredibly swift movement, Roger smashed his right elbow against Butolo's jaw, then slammed his fist down against Butolo's wrist, not breaking it, but causing the muscles of the islander's hand to spasm. Roger flicked the knife away.

The young man's spear had already broken in the fall.

Roger lay atop him for just a few seconds more, to show that Butolo had no more fight. Then Roger stood up and backed off. His own chest heaving, Roger leaned over and offered a hand of friendship.

The crowd was stunned into silence. There was no sound until Butolo, having wiped the blood from his lips and apparently willed the frown from his face, accepted the hand. Roger helped him to rise from the earth. Butolo opened his arms and embraced Roger, slapping him on the back. It was over. Roger had proven himself. He could take part in the action against the false sun-priests.

Great.

The people who had surrounded them at a distance now rushed forward, cheering the two fighters. Roger was working hard to come back from his nightmare. He attempted to find the strength and the vision to smile, then to accept pumping handshakes. But he was careful to keep Butolo near, never allowing any impression that he had contempt for the man he'd defeated. He didn't. He couldn't feel contempt toward someone who clearly possessed the competence and the will to kill him.

There was a strange sensation of cloth around Roger's shoulder—his father's arm. Roger looked over and saw Michael's smile. Suddenly all the fantasy and all the nightmare disappeared. He grabbed hold of Michael and wanted to lose himself in his father's grip. "Oh shit, Dad, that was fucking horrible."

"But you won. I never doubted it. You won."

He had won. Roger was proud of it. He had come clean on the first real assignment in the field, and he'd done it alone. But there was a nagging doubt in his mind.

But if I hadn't. I'd be dead. You would have let them kill me.

And even when Roger pulled back and looked his father directly in the eye, he knew this was so.

25

LAO CHIANG WAS more perturbed than his daughter was used to seeing him. "There was a disruption during a service the other evening," he said quickly, ignoring the pleasantries they would usually exchange. "I've lost Meking."

"Lost him?" Lin Tao asked. "The natives surely didn't turn on him? We've only been dealing with the most placid—"

"Yes, yes, I know that. Someone, I don't know who, barged in on the service. Their bodies were found. They'd been shot. One of them had been tortured."

She frowned at that. "What might he have said?"

She was still bothered by the way that Occidental youngster had responded to that mask. Her father was right. People on the coast shouldn't be able to recognize it.

"We'll have to move up the service. Word of this will get out. We have the village of Leittar in our hands. We can't take the chance of their slipping. The whole operation demands that we take our time, and we have a certain leeway for mistakes—but we could not afford to begin all over again."

"Then we'll move the ceremony," Lin Tao answered. She smiled. "I enjoy the ceremonies."

"You've taken to them very well, daughter. I had thought that your entertainments were sufficiently extreme to release your urges."

Lin Tao shrugged. "The boys who come from the cruise ships and the students are occasionally interesting enough. But not always."

"Don't let your escapades interfere with your tasks. You know as well as I that the Tong will give us freedom to do whatever we choose, so long as our job is fulfilled. But if we fail, it's our lives. There's no forgiveness . . ."

"I know that as well as you do," Lin Tao answered. The violent revenge that the international crime syndicate called the Tong could extract was legendary. They were cruel, relentless, utterly without mercy.

When Chinese settlers had first came to America they had thought that they had escaped the clutch of the Tong. They had watched with light pleasure as the Americans decried the presence of the Mafia, the Italian equivalent. But there was no real equating of the two. Compared to the Tong, the Mafia looked like a bunch of bullying children, strutting in a schoolyard.

But it wasn't long before the Tong's reach extended to North America. Its first assignment was to get to those foolish Chinese who thought that coolie camps and new names would be enough—with seven thousand miles of ocean—to escape the rule of the dreaded lords of the underworld. That fancy was quickly erased when the ritual murders began in New York, San Francisco, and other cities. That had been a century ago. Now the Tong was in place in all the United States cities, allowing the Italians and other minor crime syndicates to go about their noisy parochial business while the Tong quietly continued its global enterprises.

The Tong moved with the ages. Politics meant minor disruptions. New migrations of the people they ruled only opened new markets. Chinese in America? Then the need for opium and heroin would be increased.

Now there was a new disruption. It was larger. But the warning had been given. 1999. That was the date. By then the work of Lao Chiang and Lin Tao would have to be completed. When it was—and it would be, or father and daughter would have died trying—they would reap rewards to satisfy the power-lust of an Alexander and the greed of a Midas.

26

"SO WHY DON'T YOU let the Marines do it?" Sheila asked. "Let them bring the Phantom jets and the tanks and the whole works and you can let them take care of it all. Whatever 'it' is."

They were in the guest hut that had been assigned to them. Not far distant was the noise of the banquet. After the speeches, and the food, and the first several rounds of liquor, the adults had risen and departed, leaving the young people to cavort unmolested. Michael listened to the noise, hearing, occasionally, Roger's laugh. He and Butolo were now best friends, just as the tradition dictated.

Michael turned to Sheila. She was a good-looking woman. More than good enough. Tension was shot through Michael's body. He never wanted to go through anything like this day again. But some part of him knew it would happen—often. Too often he'd see his own son in mortal combat with a worthy opponent who would be more than capable of ending this dream of their lives led together.

It was, somehow, that tension that was forcing him to see Sheila anew. Her breasts were heavy and fleshy. He knew they'd have those flat, large nipples, the kind that don't get very erect, but are surrounded with a huge expanse of pink flesh.

He'd like that, right now. He moved over to her.

Michael seldom misjudged a woman's interest. He

was sure he wasn't misjudging Sheila's. It was the kind of interest a man didn't have to worry about, because there was nothing in it about marriage, the rest of time, or even tomorrow. Sheila was a woman who'd been around, who wanted a man's embrace but had no time for the bullshit that might come with it.

She was his female mirror. He knew it. He reached and dragged on her hair, just slightly. He pulled her toward him.

They kissed. There was no resistance on her part. Then she pulled back. "You looking for more than a pilot, Sheriff?"

He didn't answer with words but led her to the mat in the corner. They sprawled on it and quickly removed their clothing, just helping one another often enough that their movements couldn't be sensed as mechanical or desperate.

Naked, Michael moved onto Sheila. He was hard— and Sheila was ready, because he slid into her easily. They made love slowly, lingeringly, their tongues met and explored.

Her hands gestured and immediately Michael understood. Without leaving her he rolled onto his back, bringing her with him, and let her set the speed: slow, slow, slow. She lifted herself up and then gradually slid back onto his erection. Those breasts were just as he had imagined. They were heavy and hung down, still firm, but swinging pendulously as she rocked.

Sheila lifted up her head, staring without seeing through the open side of the hut at the inky tropical sky, her mouth open with a silent groan of pleasure. Michael clenched his teeth, not moving, letting her take her pleasure, enjoying her hands pressed on his chest, her fingers clutching at him. She pulled at his chest hair, holding on as she continued to ride him.

Suddenly her hot and wet rubbing got to be too much for Michael. He reached up and pulled on her shoulders, forcing her to acknowledge him. She leaned over, still holding on, and they kissed again, hungrily. She moved slightly, spreading her legs, and Michael had an even more pleasurable angle as he began to pump his hips into her, meeting her own drives.

They kept their mouths open and on one another even after they'd passed the time for kissing. They could hear and feel the groans building up inside them as they pulsed further and faster. Then Michael sensed Sheila's scream deep in his own throat. Just once more, harder, harder than any time before and he orgasmed fiercely, just as her muscles clamped hot around him.

"I still want to know why you don't just call in the Marines," Sheila commented a while after their lovemaking had ended.

Michael lay flat on his back, legs spread apart in repose. Sheila leaned over him, playing with the curls of hair over his crotch.

"They'd just get lost in the jungle." His answer evidently bothered her, for she stopped her hand and stared down at him.

"What's going on, Sheriff? In Suparta? You seem to know. What's this game you're playing with the natives? That kid you brought along with you is a student assistant the way I'm a bridesmaid. I don't get it."

He didn't look her in the eye, he just stared straight up into the blackness of the thatched roof. He listened to the laughing and occasional singing at the banquet, at last dying down.

"This country's a fake," he said. "It's all facade. Jungle facade. Resort facade. I don't *know* what's going on. What do you think? You've lived here most of your life. Why haven't other people come in here, to the interior, found these people?"

Sheila shrugged. "Why should they? I mean, the jungle's too thick for cultivation. The people aren't warlike. The government isn't threatened. There's no reason to come in here. They get schooling, the hospital's close by—"

"That's just it. Don't you see? This is a whole lot of fakery on their part. These people have chosen to live this life. They send in some of their sons to the cities. Do you realize that Butolo went to the university—probably got a better education than"—he nearly said *my son* but caught himself—"than Roger is getting, but after that he came back here to live the rest of his life in a loincloth? That's pretty amazing. But only if you don't understand what's really going on—and I obviously don't.''

"That guy who fought Roger? A university graduate? You've got to be kidding."

"No," said Michael. "He came clean about it after the fight. Roger'll have even more information before the night's over, if he doesn't get drunk on the sugar liquor they're pouring down his throat."

Sheila shook her head, smiled down at Michael.

He went on: "It's a well-thought-out deception. Well organized and well planned. But something's gone wrong with it. That's the only possible reason why they're willing to take us in and let us be a part of the struggle. This is—I bet—one of the most closed societies in the world."

She lay down beside him again, arranging her breasts so that they rested heavily across his chest.

"I know of others." said Michael, "other societies that fight desperately against outside forces to keep them from infiltrating, that or else keep them from diluting some native magic or superstition. But these people are much, much smarter. They haven't just closed themselves off, they've created something much more powerful—they're consciously and intelligently putting on an act."

"Why?" Sheila asked quietly, as her hand inched lower down Sheriff's naked torso.

"It has to do with the temples and the religion," Michael answered. "There's something upsetting their balance of power, something they're disturbed by. It's the only explanation of why they would let us in. They have an outside enemy and they need an outside ally to help overcome it.''

''You just don't know who the enemy is,'' said Sheila.

''Right.''

She laughed, and grabbed him hard. ''Just like I don't know who *you* are.''

27

THE NEXT MORNING Michael went to the hut that Roger was sharing with Butolo. Both young men were there, naked, with two young naked women. On seeing them, all the worry that Michael had once had about Roger's sense of privacy was gone—disappeared. An unconcern with sex and bodily functions came with this territory, this tropical Eden that was as beautiful as the tourist brochures claimed it to be. Except that few tourist brochures promised group sex.

Michael just ignored the sleeping young people and stared around the village. It was well maintained. The grounds were kept up by the children, every day cutting back the incursions that the forest had made. Over to the west Michael could see the red edge of the island's central plateau as it rose from the mass of greenery. Up there were the satellite tracking stations—and the corpses of the New Zealand scientists.

Michael could see Sheila's helicopter parked on the outskirts of the clearing. It was strange that the modern machinery didn't look out of place in the village, and it was even stranger that it had attracted so little attention when they'd landed. That should be a clue to something. But what? Why hadn't the children been frightened? Why hadn't the adults been intrigued and curious? Whenever he'd been to a village this isolated, a machine like the 'copter would have drawn awe from the populace.

Here, it was simply viewed as an interesting mode of

transportation. It wasn't out of place . . . perhaps because it was a familiar mode of transportation?

Michael Sheriff looked over to a group of nearby children. In front of them stood a man and a woman, wearing traditional garb, a loincloth for the man, a wraparound skirt for the woman. But they were holding classes for attentive and appreciative children. There weren't any Western tools—no printed books, no fancy gimmicks, no overhead projectors.

If you have children that want to learn and who have all along been taught that learning is a good thing, you don't need tricks to hold their attention. Sheriff remembered all the subterfuges that teachers were using in the States to interest the bored and the misbehaving. Tools for spoiled brats who stayed in school only because they wanted to go to college where they could drink beer and get laid, and put off responsible adulthood for another four years.

But these kids, they were studying with the intent and purpose of initiates into some religious order. Then Sheriff realized something else—the lesson for today *was* the helicopter. By the motions they made, it was clear to Michael that the two adult teachers were showing the children how the bird lifted straight up off the ground.

Jesus! No wonder they weren't in awe of the thing. These eight-year-olds were getting training in aerodynamic theory.

"Mr. Sheriff."

Michael turned to see an English-speaking native standing beside him. The man spoke with an educated accent. This wasn't pidgin.

"The elder would like to speak to you."

"I'd like to talk to him myself," Michael said.

The two men strode across the clearing to the elder's hut. Michael asked, "Does the elder speak English?" Michael knew well from experience that not everyone who employs an interpreter actually needs one.

Caranti smiled. "He honestly doesn't. You could

speak Dutch to him if you like. But few Americans, I realize—''

''I know Dutch,'' said Sheriff.

The old man was waiting for them, cross-legged in the dirt just within the shade cast by the roof of his hut.

''Do you enjoy our village?'' the old man asked in his native tongue. His younger companion translated.

''I'm intrigued by it,'' replied Sheriff in Dutch.

The elder smiled when he heard the answer. ''What do you think of us?'' he asked again, this time in Dutch.

''I think you're all actors. I think you're pulling the wool over everyone's eyes.''

The elder didn't respond to the accusation. ''I have watched you,'' he said. ''Watched you and your son. How you have quickly made yourself—or how you have tried to make yourself—a part of our people. Your son even now is sleeping with one of my granddaughters. He is the friend of my grandson. He is proven. I have chosen to trust you.''

The elder's Dutch was formal and courtly, as if he had learned it out of an old-fashioned textbook, which didn't seem unlikely.

''I think you've decided that you have to trust me,'' said Sheriff.

''Yes. I have to trust you. Would you like a history lesson?''

''Yes.'' There were obviously going to be no direct answers here. Sheriff knew to take what he could get.

''When the Europeans came to Suparta, we saw that we could not overcome them, so we chose not to fight. Some of our people—mostly the ones on the coast—became Europeanized. Others chose to stay in the jungle. Those on the coast became Christianized. We kept to the old gods, though by then—on our own—we had given up human sacrifice, and the solemn practice of eating our defeated enemies.''

This much Sheriff already knew, and he nodded. *Go on. Get to the interesting part.*

"The two groups have evolved. Our own, those who stay in the interior, have even developed a new class. It came from the oldest and the most honored caste of priests. Do you know what it is?"

"No."

"They are referred to as 'Monitors.' " The old man spoke this single word in English, and Sheriff couldn't imagine where the term had originated. "They are the ones, like Butolo, who go to the settlements and study the ways of the other people: the other Supartans and the Europeans and Americans and Asians who come to our island. They keep track of things that could alter the way we live. They must take vows, much like priestly vows, before they leave."

"Why don't they stay?"

"Because the jungle is their home. Because in Sutaka and Pato Lako and the islands and cities beyone they are little. Because here in the jungle they are our leaders. I was a Monitor in my youth. I am Headman of Trali now."

"Why don't they bring back more? More civilization?" Sheriff wasn't arguing, but he needed to know.

"Civilization? What is civilization? Transportation? In the jungle there is nowhere to go but to the next village, and the easiest quickest way is on foot. Is it medicine? We have a doctor here, and he has the drugs necessary to vaccinate our children. Do we need an architect here? Every adult in Trali has the ability and strength to build a new house when a storm tears one down. Communications? Our messengers would have nothing to do. Agriculture? Food grows in the jungle without our having to plant it." The old man shrugged as if he could go on in this vein for some time.

"We chose, our ancestors chose, long ago, to maintain our way of living, our gods, our society. We like many things about ourselves. Other people fought the Europeans, and were enslaved or exterminated. When they did not fight they were assimilated, and their children became neither this nor that.''

"Like the people in Pato Lako and Satuka?''

"They can live their lives. But we choose not to join them.''

Sheriff pondered for a few moments. "But what has happened? Why are you opening up now?''

"We are not opening up,'' said the leader. "I am merely giving you a lesson in history.''

That wasn't the answer and Sheriff knew it.

After a moment the old man went on, "The government wants the interior settled. The factories on the northern shore are a success. They make money. They bring prestige on the government. The prime minister would like more factories, and would like to go deeper into the jungle.''

"The island is large,'' said Sheriff. But the old man didn't even bother to respond to this—for he knew, as did Sheriff, that the first incursion signified many more to come.

"Our women, who should be raising children, and should be teaching their children the old ways, are now shut in factories. They purchase television sets,'' he added with contempt.

"But Eyes of the Sun—and human sacrifices—will bring them to their senses,'' said Sheriff with grim irony.

"No!"

"They are your totems, your rituals,'' Sheriff pointed out. "If not you, then who is doing this?''

The old man didn't reply to the question directly. Sheriff thought he was not being evasive—he simply didn't know the answer.

"We have no central government in the interior. Our traditions don't even allow for land ownership among the members of a village population. Food, land, all of it is abundant, but it takes the work of all for the land to be cleared, and the food to be gathered. Our villages stand apart from each other, and our people come together on only two occasions each year. A Festival of the Sun, and a Festival of the Moon. That is when marriages are arranged. Our people marry outside their villages. Wives travel, and sons do not.'' The old man went suddenly silent.

Sheriff tried to make the leap of logic that the headman seemed to expect of him.

''You believe there is an intrusive element here in the interior.''

''Yes.''

''And you don't know who it is?''

''I do not.''

''Do you think that it has something to do with the religion?''

''That is obvious.''

''What are you afraid of?''

''I do not know. If it is an outsider who is doing this, you may be able to understand his motives. I do not. I do not believe it is interior people who are making human sacrifices. I believe it is false priests. But priests hide behind rituals and masks, and we do not know their faces.''

''When is the next gathering?'' Sheriff wanted to know.

''The Festival of the Moon. In three weeks.''

. . . 28

ALWAYS THE QUESTION presented itself: what to do next?

The old man had an idea. "Butolo's sister is married to a villager where there have been more and more secrets lately. If Butolo went there, using the excuse of his new brother, perhaps he could help us."

"Use the boys?" Michael Sheriff swore beneath his breath.

The elder was startled. "Boys? They are *men*. You yourself called your son a man, and sent him into combat to prove it. It they are men, then it is time for them to take on a man's responsibility. Butolo and your son have an excuse to travel. The news of the hand-to-hand combat, of the new relationship with an off-islander. And the off-islander's desire to see the villages of his new home-land—"

"Yes, yes, of course," Michael said quickly, hardness in his voice. "Roger has every reason to go with Butolo." Michael turned and saw his son, dressed in a loincloth, wearing only the paint of a Supartan native, and remembered himself in Africa, painted blue by his fellow warriors of Leikawa. He had been led by them into a private hell of himself, his dreams, his own violence and hatred. Roger would one day have to experience that. He looked then at Butolo, a tall, intelligent, handsome Supartan youth. At least Roger would have a good companion.

* * *

Roger was pleased with the assignment, for it implied his father's trust in his abilities. Michael Sheriff even had the good grace to refrain from saying, "I don't have any other choice."

Roger was less happy when he was told that he would have to leave all his equipment behind, and travel through the jungle with nothing but spear and knife. He would never pass for a native Supartan, but he had to look vulnerable if he was going to be of any use as a reconnoiterer.

The journey to the next village was a full morning's trek, but Butolo and Roger took the route easily, stopping at a pool to bathe. To Roger's disgust, Butolo speared two very fat and greasy-looking black frogs and then roasted them over a small fire. Roger's hunger overcame his repulsion, however, and though he longed for the packages of freeze-dried beef, he devoured the crispy haunches of the two smoking amphibians.

They reached the next village late in the afternoon. The village's name was Leittar. Butolo presented himself to the headman and introduced his brother Roger. Then the two young men went in search of Butolo's sister, who they found waiting silently for them before her cooking fire.

She bowed to Roger, exchanged some brief sentences with Butolo, and then went to fetch her husband. This man and Butolo were already acquainted, of course, but there was evidently no love lost between them. Dinner was a silent, uncomfortable affair, arranged around the fire, and afterward, there was no conversation before sleep.

Morning brought no improvement, either in the hut of Butolo's sister or in the village at large. No one would speak to the two young men voluntarily, and even when Butolo pressed, replies were brief and uncommunicative.

Roger and Butolo retreated to a place on the edge of the jungle where they could speak without being overheard. This part of the business wasn't going well. His father had sent them out for information, and he hadn't found out anything except that the natives were un-friendly. And boring. He was just glad that he wasn't trying this alone, that he had Butolo for support and companionship.

Roger shook his head at his own thoughts. *Just a couple of guys . . .* Less than two years ago just a couple of guys would be hanging around the strip in Reno, drinking beer they'd persuaded a wino to buy for them, talking about skirts, themselves in designer jeans and some T-shirt with a filthy slogan on it.

Now? Now just a couple of guys were sitting around in the dirt with greasy yellow paint on their faces, wearing only a thin loincloth with their asses hanging out, sipping on lethal sugar liquor that was creating a buzz more than anything a six-pack of Bud would ever give them.

I'm just one of the guys . . .

Roger liked Butolo. He liked him a lot. The other male was quick and strong and laughed at good jokes. Roger was amazed at how close they had become in a very short time. He knew, instinctively, that it was because of the fight. That and the shared adventure of this investigation. They had to be friends; they had fought cleanly and Roger had won. Now, when they fought, they'd both have to win, or else they'd both lose, and it wouldn't be just a matter of pride.

Butolo handed Roger the carved container of sugar liquor. "My sister is acting strangely," he said. Roger was always startled, even now, with the fluency of Butolo's English. It was better English than some of the guys Roger had known back in Reno. He had to remind himself that this man, with the round face of all Polynesians—an attribute that Americans connected with simplemindedness—was a college graduate. He was also a Monitor, something he took great pride in.

Roger figured it wasn't too different from his own case. Learn a skill, a lot of skills, that made you potentially very powerful. Then enter a society and hide your skills, hold down that tendency to show yourself off. Sit and wait until the moment you're needed, then activate your strength fast and hard. Wasn't that the formula for an MIS agent as well as a Monitor? It made sense to Roger. The only thing was, he hadn't prepared himself to find a peer in the jungles of Suparta.

"How long since you've seen your sister?" Roger asked his friend.

"Not long. A month. But she is suspicious of something."

"Me, probably."

"Maybe. But she has seen westerners before. And she knows the tradition of brother-making."

"Does she know you're a Monitor?"

"Of course."

Roger thought about this for a few minutes. Then he said, "Look, I realize there's a hell of a lot that I don't know about you and your people, but in the place where I grew up, when a woman gets married her allegiance changes. Her old family is less important than her husband."

"Yes," said Butolo, as if the concept were not entirely foreign.

"And maybe *his* village becomes *her* village," suggested Roger.

"Oh, yes," Butolo confirmed. "That is true."

"Your grandfather suspects this village of being in league with the false priests." Butolo nodded. "The false priests are telling the people to kill westerners, isn't that what your grandfather also thinks?"

"Yes," said Butolo, then added after a moment, "Brother, I think it is time we left this village."

But by then it was too late, for at that moment the two young men felt the sharpened points of spear blades against their backs.

29

SHEILA LOOKED ON intently as Michael Sheriff stalked his hotel room. He seemed to be a caged beast. That was it: some kind of wild animal who didn't have a clear target to attack. She wondered vaguely what it would be like to see him do that, see him really take on an enemy with this sort of energy seeping from every pore.

The telephone rang. Sheriff nearly ripped it from the wall as he answered it, pulling so hard at the cord. "Yes."

This end of the conversation was just monotones. "Yes." "No." "What?" "Yes." "Where?" Sheriff finally hung up, with no hint of politeness at the end of the call.

He sat down on the bed and put his head in his hands.

"So?" Sheila had waited as long as she could before pressing him for information.

Sheriff looked up quickly, as though surprised to see her there still. He relaxed his shoulders with obvious concentration. "It makes no sense. Any usual reason for this sort of thing happening doesn't compute here. There are no strategic mineral deposits on the island. There's a real benefit to the tracking stations, but the government hasn't barred any other country from taking part in those benefits—if the Russians wanted to set up here, they probably could. And if the point was to kill all the installations, why start with the New Zealanders, and why *stop* there? There's no organized opposition party of any con-

186

sequence, and no unorganized anarchists who do violence for the sake of violence.''

Sheriff stood and walked over to the window of his hotel room. Directly below was the pool. Flabby, sunburned Americans were drinking, making belly-flop dives, flirting. Roger, covered with yellow paint, was a hundred miles away in the jungle. Alive, his father hoped.

''What does that leave you with?'' Sheila prompted.

''That leaves us with an interior subculture on this island. A culture that was invisible. The headmen and the villagers have their own way to escape westernization of Suparta. Yes, there's the encroachment of the government-sponsored villages in the north, but so far that's minute. The resentment is only at a stage of ill-defined anger.''

He turned and looked at Sheila, as if wanting confirmation of his analysis. ''There is no reason in the world for anyone to disrupt this country. None. There is no reason for those sacrifices, there is no reason . . .''

''Sounds like religion to me,'' Sheila said with disgust. ''Whenever you find something that is evil and doesn't make sense, seems like there's a missionary not far behind.''

''But even that,'' Sheriff said with exasperation, ''isn't making any sense. The false priests that the elder talked about just don't register. If they were trying to foment an anti–Western revolution, if they were trying to set up a new government to take over the island's strategic geography, then we could go for the source—the party that was going to benefit. But there's no benefit, and the religion itself would be in trouble if the prime minister intervened with troops. There's just nothing to be *gained* . . .''

''There's a resource all right,'' said Sheila. ''And it sure as hell does have something to do with religion. You got to understand, Sheriff. I was married, twice as it happens, but this is about my first husband. A real hellraiser, and one of the best lays I ever had. That is, until his daddy came home and pulled in the rope. Daddy was a Mormon missionary, the worst kind. He had that man of mine walking the tight and narrow in a matter of days. All of a sudden, all the really fun things we had been doing in bed were the devil's work—I think that old bastard must have gotten my husband to *confess* his sinful goings-on. After that, sonny-boy was a cipher, a real puppet. That's what I see when I see religion. Control."

Sheriff said nothing.

"A controlled population is a way to a government. There's that. There's someone who can get something out of Suparta that has to do with that. Someone who wants a government and who wants people. People are the resource."

"All this for a passive labor force?" It wasn't computing in Sheriff's mind. "All this for an island that . . ."

He knew there had to be some force involved that wasn't in the computers and which wasn't computing in his own mind. The hotel room felt like a trap. There was no place to go to fill in the gaps. No information that could be added—and yet he knew something was missing. He slammed a fist against the wall. What was the element they had overlooked?

30

Roger and Butolo sat next to one another on the edge of the great center circle of the village of Leittar, just two more of the two or three hundred gathered there. But different of course, because Roger and Butolo had their hands tied behind them, and the knots were staked to the ground. Their crossed legs were similarly bound.

The postion was an uncomfortable one in the hot sun, for there was no way of wiping away the sweat that poured down their faces. No way of avoiding the reddish dust that blew into their eyes and mouths. No way of relieving the cramps they suffered in their bound limbs.

No way of avoiding the fear of what was to come.

It was late afternoon, still hot, but already the villagers of Leittar had started a great fire in the middle of the circle and it was burning bright and hot.

Butolo's sister sat directly across the circle from them, hidden by the pyre, but once when she'd gotten up to fetch something from her husband, Butolo exchanged a glance with her.

"She is sorry," he whispered to Roger. "But there is nothing that she can do."

The man next to Butolo whacked him across the face for the whispering, and on the other side, Roger was whacked for having listened.

The drums were beating, too, somewhere behind the two young men. The drums shook the ground and made the blood in their veins jump with the rhythm. The noise

189

produced the kind of headache that a world full of aspirin wasn't going to cure.

Inside the ring of villagers were the totems that Roger had seen from the helicopter. Now he could see them up close. Colorful yarn arranged in geometric patterns on a framework of sharpened sticks. Kindergarten stuff. All the totems were red and yellow and blue and green— except for the two that were stuck into the earth in front of Roger and Butolo. These had been held over the fire for a moment. The colorful yarn had flared and charred, and now they stood in the earth like broken black spiders' webs.

That little piece of symbolism didn't seem to bode well for Roger and his friend.

Roger realized now why the village had been so unwelcoming to him and Butolo. This was the sort of ceremony that had long been planned. The two outsiders interfered—but now, of course, he and Butolo were part of it.

An integral part, maybe.

The sinking of the sun behind the forest trees was a signal for an intensification of the ritual. The drums grew louder—that hadn't seemed possible—and more erratic in their rhythms. At the same time several small bales of green wood were tossed on the fire, causing it to flare and crackle and spark. The villagers began to chant, an old slow chant that was out of sync with the drums. Four hollowed-out gourds suddenly appeared in the circle of villagers now, and were passed both left and right. Every second or third person—man, woman, and child— sipped from it and passed it on. This was done at such a pace, with the gourds traveling in different directions, that it all began to look like a conjurer's trick.

Roger's curiosity about the drink was soon satisfied. Several times the gourds passed them by, going in both directions, but once suddenly, the man next to him grabbed Roger's jaw, pried open his mouth, and poured in a large splash of the liquid. It was bitter but Roger swallowed it before he knew what had happened—he'd had nothing liquid for the last six or seven hours. A few moments later Butolo got the same treatment.

Night came on quickly, as it does in the tropics. The bonfire still burned, the drums beat, the villagers swayed and chanted. All of it was timeless, hypnotic, and—in its way—comforting. Roger began to lose the sense of danger, simply because nothing new was happening. All day there had been the fire, the drums, and the chanting. Now it was dark, and there was still the fire, the drums, and the chanting. For the past several hours there had been pressure on Roger's bladder, and suddenly the pressure was gone. He glanced down and saw the light of the fire reflected in a puddle of his own urine.

That's when he realized that he'd been drugged.

"Oh, shit," he said aloud.

Butolo looked and him and smiled. Butolo was swaying and chanting. But the totem in front of Butolo was still black and charred, and Roger knew in his heart that that meant Butolo was going to die. With that damn smile on his face, and that damn chant on his parched lips.

Oh, shit. What good was all the training in the world going to do when his mind was bent on some fucking hallucinogenic drug? What—

Roger's mind wandered away, and he was no longer thinking. He was watching the bonfire, listening to the chant, and forming the inward conviction that everybody had always been wrong on the subject of death.

Death, Roger knew now, was a pretty good thing. And the younger you got it the better. It was only the young and the strong who could appreciate death properly.

Right. That was *truth*, goddammit.

Roger was blinded with gold. He blinked. Squinted and looked again.

The limb of the golden full moon, rising over the trees.

The chanting stopped. The drums stopped. The fire burned and crackled, as if from a great distance.

All heads in the circle were turned toward the rising moon.

By infinitely small gradations, everyone of them marked in Roger's mind, the moon rose above the jungle. At the same time it shrank, it grew from gold to silver.

As it did so, the chanting and the drums began again, slowly and softly at first, growing faster and more powerful as the moon was pulled higher in the sky.

Finally, it was there, a perfect circle of silver, blindingly bright.

Then there were two of them, perfect circles of silver. One of them in the sky, the other in the midst of the circle. Hovering in the air before Roger and Butolo.

Butolo cried out in awe and despite his bonds managed to bang his forehead against the earth.

The chanting was loud, frantic.

The second moon, in the circle, was a goddess. A white robe, a circular mask of beaten silver.

Roger had seen another mask—a sun mask—and he had seen that sun mask explode with a rifle blast.

The Moon Goddess swayed with the chanting. Her movements were comforting, erotic—and familiar.

Drugs did nothing for muscular coordination, or for the operation of the will, or for the maintenance of courage—but they did improve intuition.

The Moon Goddess stood before Roger, and began a chant of her own, underlying the much louder chant of the villagers. It was hard for Roger to make out her voice, but Roger knew—without any further evidence—that beneath that silver mask was the face of Lin Tao.

SHEILA'S HELICOPTER LANDED not far from the factory. As he'd been asked to, Mr. Susaki was waiting. He was waiting patiently, and did not even look disturbed at the damage the helicopter had done to his carefully maintained lawn. Michael Sheriff climbed out of the helicopter before the rotary blades had stopped moving. Ducking over, he ran to the businessman. Sheila watched as the two men went into the building, already talking rapidly and using many hurried hand gestures.

She followed them, but didn't catch up till they were already in Susaki's office. The two were so intent on their conversation they seemed hardly to notice her.

"Impossible," Susaki proclaimed. "Why? There's no need . . ."

"What would be the most labor intensive industry that could want to move here?"

Susaki stopped suddenly. He stood and went to a map of the Pacific Basin that hung on his wall. His finger went around the mural. The countries and cities were labeled in both English and Japanese. Susaki traced a line from South Korea to Hong Kong, from there to Singapore and then back over to Taiwan. "Unstable," he said. "All of them unstable. South Korea is under constant strain from the north and from Russia. After the American abandonment of Vietnam, they don't trust you. Hong Kong is about to be relinquished by the British, and no amount of reassurance from the Red Chinese government is going to convince the capitalists that their investments will be preserved. Singapore is undergoing much stress because of the theocratic government's imposition of a strict code of personal morality. Taiwan? Would your government really go to war over that in the midst of the détente with Beijing? If it still would today, will it in another decade?''

Sheriff and Sheila stared blankly.

Susaki turned and faced them. ''Those are the governments that have benefited the most from labor-intensive industry. Their economies are the ones that produce the fabrics and the small, simple components for electronics that fuel our—and your—industries. They do it by paying wages that are lower than what would be necessary for an American—or a Japanese—laborer to survive. But all these countries are in flux. I have always thought—so have many others—that there would be an evolution toward Africa, the next frontier of unorganized labor. But no one in those industries is set up to take over a country. Some of the multinationals in our nation, or yours, are large enough to do that. I know of none that's ready to make itself an international criminal, however. There have been cases of tampering with government in both Japan and America. We both know that. But bribes to get defense contracts, payoffs to let export quotas slip—not what we're talking about in Suparta.

''For the most part, the countries involved are the places where the Japanese and the Americans are building our own plants. There are hardly any corporations in Korea or Taiwan that are owned by the nationals that could begin to compare with our organizations. They make their money off of partnerships with us.

''Only the Chinese in Hong Kong have that kind of financial power. They, of course, are among the most civilized entrepreneurs. They are also operating under a serious time constraint. When the British leave, they will leave. But they're doing it orderly. The powerful Nanking Banking Corporation just moved its headquarters to the

Caribbean and there was not a single microchip lost in the move.''

"It could just be religion," said Sheila. "Just religion gone crazy, like I saw with my first husband."

"But sun worship? Aztecs? None of it—''

Susaki cut Michael Sheriff off. "Sun worship? What a devastating symbol." He turned back to the map and looked at the Japanese islands. "The Land of the Rising Sun. What horrible things came to us because of that belief. Our emperor a god. Our land the source of light and power. All of it lost . . .''

There were pieces floating through Sheriff's mind. A puzzle so unformed that he couldn't yet even tell how large it might be.

Sheila's helicopter flew back and forth as the two of them studied the landscape below. They were zigzagging their way toward Trali. On the ground, near the American satellite dishes, they saw a collection of the Eyes of the Sun. More of them than had appeared at the New Zealand installation. Two uniformed workers were even then pulling them up out of the earth. They shaded their brows as they gazed up at the helicopter.

As soon as they had landed at Trali Sheriff and Sheila went to the elder's hut. He had heard nothing from Butolo and Roger, but assumed them still to be safe in the neighboring village.

That was one thing going well at least, thought Sheriff. Roger out of harm's way.

"Are there other temples?" Sheriff asked the old man.

"Many. None as large as the Temple of the Sun, of course."

Sheriff thought for a while. "Which others are in use now? Do you know?"

"Three, four of them that I hear about. But only rumors. Only my suspicions."

"We have to investigate all of them. Can you read a Western map?"

The old man shook his head. ''Western maps are inaccurate. I will have to tell Caranti, and Caranti will travel with you. The nearest is the Temple of the Moon. You will go there tomorrow.''

''Sooner,'' said Sheriff.

''We can fly,'' Sheila said. ''There's a searchlight mounted on the front of the 'copter. And tonight is the full moon anyway.''

. . . 32

THE TEMPLE OF THE MOON wasn't far. It couldn't have been far, considering the drugged state of most of the villagers. A procession tramped through the jungle. Just before they'd set off, with torches, Roger and Butolo were given more of the gourd-drug. Butolo swallowed the liquid off almost eagerly, and Roger pretended to, but he kept it at the back of his throat and, in the movement and darkness, managed to spit it out again.

Yet some had seeped down into his stomach, or entered his bloodstream through the lining of his throat, for he felt that lightheadedness. He came in and out of consciousness of his situation.

The two friends were near the end of the procession. Because the jungle path had already been trampled in by those moving ahead, their progress was easy. The Moon Goddess walked a few meters ahead. Roger realized that he must have been mistaken in identifying her as Lin Tao. The same height, the same shape, yes—but it couldn't be the woman he'd fucked on the beach. Twice. What the hell would she be doing in a get-up like that? What the hell would she be doing here?

The temple suddenly hove into view. Just a small place, gleaming white in the moonlight, with the salt flats surrounding it. The trees overhung on every side so that it must have been nearly impossible to see it from the air. It was also in much better condition than the other temple, where the hearts had been laid out on the altar. It still had its roof, the walls has been scrubbed of algae and fungus, the painted figures—large versions of the Eye of the Sun—were still bright and gleaming.

All the patterns were red.

Blood red.

"Butolo—" Roger hissed.

But as Butolo's head turned toward him, everything went black—everything but a bright point of light at the very back of Roger's head.

That's where I've been hit.

When he came to, Roger didn't care that he was naked, and that the whole village was arranged before him. He didn't even feel much pain, and he speculated that he'd had some more of that drug poured down his throat while he was unconscious. He could barely feel the dull ache where he'd been struck, and the temple stone at his back should have been cold and clammy, but he could scarcely feel it at all.

He looked over at Butolo and knew that his new best friend was in even worse condition. Whatever they'd been given was wild. This must be what PCP was like. He'd heard about the effects of angel dust. Sometimes hallucinogenic, very mellow, mellow beyond belief. This was a mellow drug, it had to be, because here he was naked, weaponless, tied in a spread-eagle to a blood-stained temple wall, and he wasn't particularly upset about it.

Here he was, big bad MIS agent, nude and hurting, vulnerable and blitzed on some drug. He wondered if the young women of Leittar found him a turn-on. He wanted to ask Butolo about it. But he couldn't seem to move his mouth. No, no way could he move his mouth. It flapped when he opened it, but no sound came up from his lungs.

Butolo, old buddy, he would have said, *we're in deep shit.*

Then Roger started to cry. He was so damned happy to

have Butolo as a friend, and now it struck him how lonely he'd been. There he was, losing Stasia and not knowing the nerds at Breslauer, and his old man was a fucking MIS agent, too, and he hadn't had a friend in so long, just somebody to hang with, and suddenly here was Butolo, and goddamn it, these two friends were going to die together. Fucking give up the fucking ghost. Except they were going to get out of it. Somehow. They'd be best friends for the rest of their lives. He'd move to Suparta so he could stay with his buddy. They'd go fishing. Fuck Breslauer, fuck MIS. Even his father would be happy to have him safe and sound on a tropical paradise of an island, just fishing with his buddy, planking some native girls together. It'd be great, just great.

He wanted to tell Butolo that's what was going to happen. Just the two of them and maybe sometimes they'd meet Roger's dad in Pato Lako for Christmas. They'd go hunting together, and they'd get girls and that would be a great life. Fuck civilization, just the way Butolo's people always had.

He tried to make his mouth move to tell Butolo the words. But even if he could have gotten his mouth to work it would have been too late. Because by the time Roger got his mouth open, the Moon Goddess—her silver mask shining in the bright moonlight—had walked up with a long curved knife and dragged it across Butolo's throat.

A long stream of blood pulsed a gleaming black out of the wound.

One, two, three, four, five.

Roger counted the pulses, each weaker than the last. Then the blood was only seeping gently out of the dead man's throat. Butolo's head, with the eyes staring and sad, sagged toward Roger.

Tears flowed down Roger's cheeks. *Goddamn, it happened again.*

The Moon Goddess stood before Roger. Her white

robe now bore a diagonal of blood—the first dying pulse out of Butolo's neck.

She stood, cold and impassive.

Roger looked behind her. The village of Leittar was ranged about. He could see pinpoints of light in their eyes—they were looking up at the moon, and not at him.

The only noise was that of a solitary woman weeping. *Butolo's sister,* Roger thought.

No other noise.

The Moon Goddess stepped forward and raised the blade of the bloody knife.

Crack.

A noise that was sharp and familiar and welcome—a rifle shot.

The Moon Goddess seemed to shudder.

Crack.

She toppled forward, slashing downward with the knife.

Instinctively, Roger lurched his body to the right and just saved his belly from being ripped open by the weapon.

The villagers screamed and shouted, but their confusion was dampened by the drugs. A few more shots, and then everyone was running. A man running toward Roger was shot down instantly, and twitched on the salted floor.

The Moon Goddess had fallen against Roger's knees, but his senses were so drug-dampened he could hardly feel her as she dragged herself upward.

Her metallic mask pressed cold against his naked thigh, and then slipped off.

He looked down.

Lin Tao.

"WORDS OF ONE SYLLABLE," said Maxwell Barton. "That's about all the boys in Washington can understand."

"Now is not the time," said Sheriff. Because this was a hospital corridor, and Roger was inside one of these rooms, and Michael *had* to know his condition.

The ambassador shrugged. "You can't go in there yet anyway. Make it quick and I'll get out of your life. If you'll get out of mine."

"Lao Chiang will spill all the fine details. He's got to be scared shitless after all this. His life's not worth a copper penny if you guys don't pull one of your new identity numbers on him. That won't even do much good."

"The witness protection plan works," said Barton. "We can hide him even if we have to de-slant his eyes."

"Not from other Chinese. Not from the ones who are going to be looking for him."

"Out with it, Sheriff. Give it to me fast. If I know the outline, I can get that guy to paint by the numbers and give me a big picture later."

"MIS and even you guys, the CIA, deal with the big pictures. We think in terms of nations and revolutions, multinationals and strategic mineral despoits. We think big. We also think in terms of a set of factors influencing the world. We're usually right. We're almost always right at MIS." He would have said *always* without the qualification before, but not now.

"Occasionally there can be something in the criminal world that enters into our calculations. A massive amount of cocaine from Colombia can mean so much money that there's a disruption in that country's economy, up or down. The banks in Miami get funny with their cash reserves. But that's small stuff. We all step in when it gets too large and we keep it in proportion.

"But there was one center that we constantly forgot to see. Hong Kong. It's the center of the drug trade, dirty money, all of it. There's been no way for the British to combat it. It was almost a constant in the world equations. There was heroin coming from the Golden Triangle in Thailand and Burma. It got distributed. We knocked out one distributorship and another popped up. That's the way it's always worked.

"There were massive amounts of money in that. But not enough to make that big a difference in what we saw. We forgot, the same people in Hong Kong also control the banks, the stock markets, all of it. They kept themselves going because they balanced it all pretty well, and because they had a whole lot of investment in the world status quo. Lose some money in drugs? Make it up in stock manipulations.

"What we forgot was that once *we* changed the status quo, then the Tong was going to have to change its operations as well. They have billions of dollars. They needed a country. A whole country.

"Suparta was perfect. They could actually grow their own poppies here. The climate, the soil, all of it would have worked for them. The little casinos in Pato Lako are just diversions for tourists now. If the Tong had gotten control, they would have become the Monte Carlo of the East.

"Hong Kong's been like a sore. It's the place where a lot of the evil and a lot of the crime in the world can fester. Keep it there and the rest of the world doesn't get infected. But we're cutting off the sore—the British are giving the colony back to the Communists. The infection had to go to a new place. So they were setting up this island—"

"The religious shit?" Barton demanded.

"The best way to disrupt the government. They had lots of options after that. They could set up puppets. But the most important thing was to make Suparta unstable. The best way to do that was to attack the superstitions of the natives in the interior. They'd done their homework. They knew what would work best. If they'd come in too heavy, they'd have to deal with the government the same way the manufacturers do. The Tong has no more desire to be regulated by Suparta's honest prime minister than it did by the Communists. Every place in the Pacific is used to a Chinese presence. Everyone in any center of power knows that there are Hong Kong Chinese of great wealth. Lin Tao—"

"Your boy's skirt?" Barton obviously enjoyed the jibe.

"Yeah." Michael Sheriff shot a hateful glance at Barton. "She could move through any social circle here. She was also putting out for the British chargé d'affaires."

"I know him," Maxwell said. "His tastes are pretty exotic."

"Anyway, they could be setting up some sophisticated stuff here in the city while they were unleashing havoc in the interior. In the end, the Tong would have had a whole new base of operations."

"Where will they go now?" Maxwell wondered.

"Somewhere. But now we'll be on the lookout for them. A whole lot of computers have just been updated with new information."

Roger burned crimson when his father came into the room.

"Jesus, I didn't know. Honest to God, I didn't know . . ."

He didn't know that he had been screwing the Goddess of the Moon on the deserted Pato Lako beach. He didn't know that he'd revealed his and Michael Sheriff's presence to the one person on the island who most needed that information. He hadn't suspected, till the very end, that it was Lin Tao who . . .

"Her cover was better than yours," said his father.

"Jesus," he said again. "What do I say?"

"You say you're a pretty lucky fuck-up, is what you say. Because you're alive, and she's dead, and that's one mistake you're never going to make again."

"No, sir."

"You feel okay?"

"I feel like shit."

"You look like shit."

They were silent for a moment. Then Michael Sheriff said, "I'm sorry about Butolo. We landed in Leittar, intending to pick you two guys up. But there was nobody in the village, so we followed the trail. If we'd gotten there two minutes earlier . . ."

Roger had closed his eyes in pain at the memory. Now he opened them again. There was a kind of hardness in his gaze that his father was both relieved and saddened to see there.

"It comes with the territory," said Roger. "Isn't that what you said."

Michael Sheriff just nodded. The kid had just learned one more lesson.

VIETNAM

A WORLD OF HURT Bo Hathaway   69567-7/$3.50 US/$4.50 CAN

A powerful, realistic novel of the war in Vietnam, of two friends from different worlds, fighting for different reasons in a war where all men died the same.

"War through the eyes of two young soldiers in Vietnam who emerge from the conflict profoundly changed...A painful experience, and an ultimately exhilarating one."

Philadelphia Inquirer

DISPATCHES Michael Herr   01976-0/$3.95

Months on national hardcover and paperback bestseller lists. Michael Herr's nonfiction account of his years spent under fire with the front-line troops in Vietnam.

"The best book I have ever read about war in our time."

John le Carre

"I believe it may be the best personal journal about war, any war, that any writer has ever accomplished."

Robert Stone (DOG SOLDIERS) *Chicago Tribune*

FOREVER SAD THE HEARTS Patricia L. Walsh   78378-9/$3.95

A "moving and explicit" (*Washington Post*) novel of a young American nurse, at a civilian hospital in Vietnam, who worked with a small group of dedicated doctors and nurses against desperate odds to save men, women and children.

"It's a truly wonderful book...I will be thinking about is and feeling things from it for a long time." Sally Field

NO BUGLES, NO DRUMS Charles Durden

69260-0/$3.50 US $4.50 CAN

The irony of guarding a pig farm outside Da Nang—The Sing My Swine Project—supplies the backdrop for a blackly humorous account of disillusionment, cynicism and coping with survival.

"The funniest, ghastliest military scenes put to paper since Joseph Heller wrote CATCH-22" *Newsweek*

"From out of Vietnam, a novel with echoes of Mailer, Jones and Heller,"

Houston Chronicle